A Castle in the Window

LAURA C. STEVENSON

CORGI BOOKS

A CASTLE IN THE WINDOW
A CORGI BOOK 0552 547190

Published in Great Britain by Corgi Books,
an imprint of Random House Children's Books

This edition published 2003

1 3 5 7 9 10 8 6 4 2

Papers used by Random House Children's Books are natural, recyclable products
made from wood grown in sustainable forests. The manufacturing processes
conform to the environmental regulations of the country of origin.

Set in 12.5/15pt Bembo by
Falcon Oast Graphic Art Ltd.

Corgi Books are published by Random House Children's Books,
61–63 Uxbridge Road, London W5 5SA,
a division of The Random House Group Ltd,
in Australia by Random House Australia (Pty) Ltd,
20 Alfred Street, Milsons Point, Sydney, NSW 2061, Australia,
in New Zealand by Random House New Zealand Ltd,
18 Poland Road, Glenfield, Auckland 10, New Zealand,
and in South Africa by Random House (Pty) Ltd,
Endulini, 5A Jubilee Road, Parktown 2193, South Africa

THE RANDOM HOUSE GROUP Limited Reg. No. 954009
www.kidsatrandomhouse.co.uk

A CIP catalogue record for this book is available from the British Library.

Printed and bound in Great Britain by
Cox & Wyman Ltd, Reading, Berkshire

To Kristine and Hanna
Auribus et manibus meis

Contents

1
Two Boxes and a Piano

Erin curled up on the window seat, looking out between the drops that slid down the window at the old-fashioned, shabby houses across the street and wishing she could disappear. Not just hide – disappear. Absolutely. Completely. Poof.

That was a dumb thing to wish, of course. Mom and Dad always said they loved her just as much as they loved Rob, who had graduated highest in his class and had a scholarship to Harvard next year. But if she were like Rob, she'd be on a plane right now, taking off for Europe with the rest of the family, instead of sitting here in Aunt Joan's house, which was as old-fashioned and shabby as the ones across the street.

Heck, she wouldn't even have had to be as super as Rob. It would have been enough if she'd passed fifth grade, like everybody else in her class. But though she'd struggled all year, her reading skills and test scores were 'considerably below grade level', so she was going to be held back. That's what the principal had said when he'd called Mom and Dad, and he'd stuck to it, even though they'd gone in together to confront him. The best they'd been able to do was get him to promise *if* Erin's reading improved from second- to fifth-grade level by fall, she could be promoted. He suggested a camp that had worked miracles with children like her, and Mom and Dad had been so happy to hear there was hope, of course she'd said she didn't want to drag around Europe anyway, and camp would be fun. Which it might have been, if she'd gotten in; but she'd been on the waiting list, and nobody had cancelled out, so at the very last minute they'd had to arrange for her to go someplace else.

Here. With Aunt Joan. She wasn't really an aunt; the Family was so complicated that kids called all the grown-ups aunt or uncle and other kids cousins. But even the grown-ups called her Aunt Joan, because everybody was so afraid of her. When Aunt Joan dis-approved of something (and she disapproved of some very ordinary things), she said so, right out, even at Family gatherings. Not always, of course, but you never knew when something was going to set her off, and even when nothing did, Mom sometimes went home upset about little things Aunt Joan had said. So when Aunt Joan had called, offering to 'take Erin over' because she'd heard from Aunt Agatha that the camp hadn't worked out, Mom had said no — at least, at first. But she'd given in, finally, because Dad said Aunt Joan might be the perfect solution; once upon a time, she'd had been some kind of teacher. Nobody had asked how many of her students had survived.

What had happened was exactly what you'd expect. At lunch today Mom had given Aunt Joan the daily schedule and a backpack of things they'd been working with and told her 'children like Erin' needed rigorously structured time, with regular activities to develop concentration span: five short reading lessons a day to aid visual perception, and several short sessions with the puzzles to build spatial abilities. Aunt Joan had smiled and nodded and said that would be fine. But the moment Mom and Dad and Rob had left for the airport, Aunt Joan had chucked the backpack into a corner and positively *stormed* at Uncle Druce over dishes. Five short reading lessons a day! Spatial abilities! Structured time! Good lord, no wonder the poor child slipped around like a ghost! Uncle Druce had pointed out that 'the poor child' was standing right there, but all that had done was turn the fire-hose of words onto her. 'The only schedule here, Erin, is breakfast at eight, lunch at twelve thirty and dinner at seven. Nobody's going to look over your shoulder all the time in *this* house! "Children like you" indeed! Every child needs freedom and privacy!' That was the end, but she'd muttered to herself even after Uncle Druce slipped away to his study.

Uncle Druce was Aunt Joan's half-brother, and there was something wrong with him. Nobody said so, but nobody had to. All the other uncles in the Family (even some of the aunts) were bankers or stockbrokers or lawyers or vice-presidents; Uncle Druce was one of the guys who collected your money if you left your car in the parking garage downtown. What's more, parking-ticket money wasn't all he collected: there were the bottle caps. The cousins said that was why he'd moved in with Aunt Joan after her husband died: the bottle caps had filled everything in his apartment but his bed. Of course you didn't believe lots of stuff the cousins said, and Erin hadn't believed that – until she'd come here.

As Aunt Joan put it this morning, the bottle caps had begun to wander out of Uncle Druce's study ten years ago, then gradually taken up residence in every corner of the house. They had. Erin looked out from behind the curtains. Except where her bed was, every wall of her room was lined with boxes labelled PEPSI or COKE with the year they'd been made. Outside the door, the little hallway that led to the stairs was lined with sagging shelves of boxed ginger ale and 7-Up caps. The shelves ended at the staircase, but the caps didn't; they were piled along the steps in boxes that took up so much space you had to go up and down very carefully. Downstairs, the walls were lined with floor-to-ceiling bookcases, all filled with special wood containers Uncle Druce had made especially for what he'd told Rob (without smiling) was the crowning glory of his collection: his beer-bottle caps. And except for a big empty space in the living room's bay window, every corner that didn't have old-fashioned, shabby furniture in it was filled with cartons, and every surface was covered with flat boxes filled with caps that hadn't been sorted yet.

Erin sighed and looked at her watch, which was digital because she couldn't tell time on a regular clock. 3:34. It had been almost two hours since she'd finished unpacking and found a place to disappear, expecting somebody to un-disappear her any minute by giving her an assignment. But Aunt Joan had apparently meant what she'd said about freedom and privacy, because nobody had even come to find her, and it looked like nobody would. *OK*, said Dad's let's-make-life-a-lesson voice in her head, *if it's 3:34, and dinner is at 7:00, how much longer will Erin have to sit here, doing nothing, before dinner?* She stared at the dial, hearing the roaring sound her ears made when her mind froze; but when she looked up, hoping to find some clue in Dad's imaginary face, all she saw was her own face in the grey glass, vibrating with the sound of a real roar.

Peering through her reflection, she saw a truck ease its way around the corner and stop just shy of a sports car parked along the side. A man in a yellow slicker jumped out of the cab, checked the sports car, made the driver back a little, then slowly, slowly, waved him on. This time, the truck cleared the car, drove down the street and stopped in front of the house. The driver jumped out and started up the walk, while the yellow-slicker guy opened the back of the truck.

Slowly, Erin spelled out the words on the side of the truck: M–C–C . . . no, words that began like that were names, so she didn't need to finish that one. M–O–V–E–R–S. A moving van, then, like she'd thought. Maybe it was coming to haul some of the bottle caps away? She tiptoed through the narrow hall and halfway down the stairs, stopping as Aunt Joan opened the front door and signed the piece of paper on the driver's clipboard. When the driver left, Aunt Joan looked up. Erin ducked back behind the banister, but it was too late.

'For heaven's sake, Erin! There's no need to hide! Come on downstairs and see what's happening. I bet you don't see a piano being moved every day.'

A piano? Erin inched down the stairs, carefully not disturbing the boxes.

Aunt Joan watched her the way people did when she was reading aloud and they were trying not to be impatient. 'It's a lovely old instrument,' she said. 'It belonged to my father, way back when. He was a concert pianist.'

Erin nodded, but the way Aunt Joan rolled her eyes said that wouldn't do for an answer in this house, so she added, 'That's nice.'

She was saved from having to say more by the two moving men, who appeared in the doorway, each carrying a large wooden box.

'Oh, right,' said Aunt Joan. 'The toy boxes. I'd forgotten all about them. Let's put them in your room,
Erin. Could you show the men where to go, to save
me the stairs?'

Erin started for the stairs, but the men, following
Aunt Joan's pointed finger, started up first. At the top,
the driver stopped and looked back. 'Right or left,
kiddo?'

Right or left. Erin looked desperately at one hand,
then the other, but there was no time to figure out
which was which; the men were waiting. 'Right,' she
said, in the confident voice she used for faking. 'All the
way at the end.'

Wrong again. Instead of turning towards her room,
the men started down the hall that went past Uncle
Druce's study and ended in the bathroom. She almost
told them to stop; then she remembered there was a
room next to the bathroom, with nothing in it but
a big window, a bed and piles of books – probably the
ones that had been taken out of the bookcases downstairs to make room for the beer-bottle caps. If the
boxes got left there now, she could move them to her
room later, and Aunt Joan would never know. So when
the men asked her if this was right, she said yes,
thank you, and began to look at the boxes, so they'd
think it was her room. You got good at covering
for yourself if you made dumb mistakes all the
time. And besides, they were pretty: old wood with
black metal corners. She was about to open one when

noises downstairs reminded her the piano was coming.

She ran to the stairs and hung over the banister, frowning as the men eased something in the door. It didn't look like a piano; it was tall, and thin, and shaped sort of like a harp. And it had wheels – or maybe that was just the thing they were rolling it on. It was hard to tell from the top. She waited until they pushed it through the living-room door, then slipped into the living room the back way, through the dining room. Nobody saw her come in; they were taking the piano's padding off.

Then she saw why it was tall and thin. It wasn't an electric piano, like the one in their apartment. It wasn't even the usual kind of real piano at school. It was a *grand* piano, standing on its side with its lid off, and inside, it did look like a harp, all gold, with thin strings running from the wide end where the keys were to pins along its beautiful curved side. The men screwed in its legs and set it up, then crawled underneath it, tightening the screws that held the pedals in place. Finally, they lifted the lid onto it, and Aunt Joan put on its music rack, and there it was – dark brown and shiny and so big it took up the whole end of the room.

'Nice piano,' said the driver. 'They don't make 'em like that any more.'

'No, they don't,' said Aunt Joan. She ran her hand over it almost as if she were stroking it, then raised the keyboard cover and played a few slightly sour notes. 'One tuning a year just isn't enough,' she said, shaking her head. 'But that's all I could persuade my step-mother to do, since nobody played it.'

The three of them walked to the front door, chatting. The piano stood in the far end of the room, making the shabby chairs look like thrones, and the unsorted bottle caps look like rubies and diamonds, as if they'd been transported to a magical castle full of knights and ladies. When Erin walked towards it, she could almost *feel* them there, waiting for a concert. She looked quickly out the door. The movers and Aunt Joan were still talking. They hadn't seen her; for all they knew, she was still upstairs.

She sat on the bench, bowed to the ghostly knights and ladies as they flocked to hear her, and began to play, her fingers charging up and down the closed mahogany keyboard cover. The knights and ladies stood transfixed, the way you did when you heard good music, so she played on until the piece in her head came to an end in three huge concluding chords, and she raised her hands high into the silent air.

'Bravo!' said a voice behind her. 'Encore!' Whirling round, she saw Uncle Druce standing in the doorway to the dining room.

She jumped up, wiping away the finger marks she'd left on the keyboard cover, and was about to apologize, but he picked up a flat box of bottle caps and shambled away. She watched him go, wondering if the way he walked was part of what was wrong with him. He was tall, like the other men in the Family, and once you got

17

used to the scruffy grey hair and the beard, you could see he looked a lot like them. But they all walked like athletes; he hardly lifted his feet, and he looked at the floor all the time. Very odd. The whole *house* was odd. The bottle caps, the people, the piano and two boxes out of nowhere . . .

The boxes! Jeez, she'd better get up there and move them. Erin rubbed the rest of her fingerprints off the keyboard cover with the bottom of her sweatshirt, started into the hall – and practically ran into Aunt Joan, who had just closed the front door.

'Oh, there you are!' said Aunt Joan. 'I was wondering where you'd gone to.'

'I was looking at the piano.'

'You *were*?' Aunt Joan frowned, and it looked like she was going to make another remark about slipping around like a ghost, but instead she asked, 'Do you play?'

'Not any more. But Rob does.'

'Well,' said Aunt Joan tartly, 'I hope he plays better than he sings. I was standing next to him last Thanksgiving – he can't carry a tune in a bucket.' She pulled a trench coat out of the closet and shoved her arms stiffly into its sleeves. 'I've got to go shopping. Would you like to come?'

'No, thank you.'

'You sure? What'll you do?'

'Look at the toy boxes.'

'Oh, of course!' Aunt Joan smiled. 'There's

wonderful stuff in them; at least, there was sixty years ago. Heaven knows what's happened to it since. OK, I'm off to buy dinner. Druce and I like chocolate ice cream with chunks. Is that OK by you?'

Obviously, she'd forgotten that Mom had said sugar was bad for children with short concentration spans, but there seemed no reason to remind her. 'Chocolate's fine.'

Aunt Joan nodded and left. Erin hurried to the room where the toy boxes were. The one nearest the door had metal handles on each side; she took one in each hand and − and nothing happened. What was in it, rocks? Well, maybe she could slide it. She pulled; it moved a little, but its metal edges left a scratch on the floor. Uh-oh. Well, maybe the other one was lighter. Nope, even worse.

Darn. She was going to have to take toys out of both of them until she could lift them, then carry the toys down to her room. She opened the heaviest box and lifted out the yellowed newspaper that covered whatever was in it. Underneath, there were blocks − but not ordinary, plastic blocks. They were made of wood, but they were the shape and colour of stones, and when you put them together right, they obviously made something special, like a house or . . . She lifted one out and looked at it. Battlements. A castle. Wow! She took out a few blocks, started to arrange them − then stopped, hearing Mom's anxious voice say *That's a great start, Erin, but*—. She sighed. She must be crazy,

19

thinking she could build a castle by herself. It was in pieces, like a puzzle – only worse, because it was three-dimensional – and she was as hopeless at puzzles as she was at reading. *If you just start in on it, you'll run into problems later on. Plan the whole thing in your head before you begin.*

She sat very still, looking at the blocks she'd laid out on the floor; then she opened the second box and took the newspaper off the top. No blocks in this one, thank heaven. Just lots of little things wrapped in tissue paper. She wiped her eyes, picked up one of them, unrolled it and stared disbelievingly at the beautiful miniature in her hand.

It was a lead knight in chain mail and a long blue cloak, carrying some musical instrument that the cloak's folds partly hid. His hair was shoulder length, and his face was so beautifully made that she could see his features – deep blue eyes like his cloak, a straight nose, high cheekbones and a wonderful, understanding smile. She smiled herself, set him carefully on one of the blocks and unrolled the next piece of tissue paper. No knight, this time: a greyhound sort of dog, standing with its head up, poised to run. It was more solid than the greyhounds you saw on leashes in the city, and it had the kind of intelligent, loyal face you'd want if you were lucky enough to have a dog of your own. She stroked its painted back and set it next to the knight. They looked perfect together.

The next few things she unrolled were benches and tables that furnished the castle she couldn't build. Then she unrolled a group of pageboys in belted blue tunics and haircuts like hers. One held a hawk, another was sharpening a dagger, a couple were carrying shields and swords; all of them looked very busy and useful. Last of all, she unrolled a black horse with armoured plates in front and on its back, and a knight's saddle on it. Rolled up with it was a knight in full armour, his legs moulded into riding position, his left hand holding a shield with a lion on it, and his right hand, down by his side, making an O. She placed him on the saddle and was admiring him when she saw a little lance lying in the tissue paper. Gently, she stuck it into the O on his hand – and there he was, all ready to ride into the lists! That was it for the first layer; there was nothing left but another piece of yellowed newspaper. But if there was one knight, there had to be more underneath. Eagerly, she peeled back the newspaper and looked.

There were knights, all right; she could see them all, because they weren't wrapped in tissue paper, just lying there, some made to go on horses, some on foot, some with pikes and battle-axes. But they looked as if they had been through a terrible battle. Some of the horses' legs were broken; others had lost their tails. The heads on the knights and foot soldiers had all been broken off, and one crimson figure was so smashed it looked as if a whole army had ridden over it. Erin gulped.

Well, of course toys got broken, and these were very delicate. She reached over into the back corner, where something was wrapped in tissue paper. As she started to unwrap it, a head fell out, then a horse's tail. She rewrapped them carefully. OK, this was a casualty ward; they were waiting to be fixed. She could do that, probably. She took out all the broken soldiers and laid them on the newspaper with the parts. Maybe Aunt Joan would have some glue or something. Meanwhile, she'd see what was underneath.

She lifted out the next layer of newspaper and stared, her hands covering her mouth. There were twenty knights and twenty horses, all dressed for battle. Once upon a time, they had been perfectly beautiful – but now, all the horses had broken legs or tails, and every knight's head was snapped off. More casualties? It seemed strange that they should all be the same sort. Gently, she lifted them out, then peeled back the next layer of newspaper. The knights on this layer wore black uniforms and carried lances with banners on them. But none of them had heads, and where their handsome black horses should have had tails, there were just stumps of grey lead. Oh, no!

Her hands shaking and her eyes blurring, Erin pulled up the corner of the next layer, then the next, then the next. But it was the same all the way to the place where the knights stopped and castle-blocks started again. There were knights, guards, squires and bowmen in each layer, all dressed in beautiful colours and equipped with swords and shields and banners and trumpets. But not one of the soldiers had a head. And every horse was broken.

2
A Castle in the Night

Dinner happened at seven, just as Aunt Joan had said it would, but it was hard to recognize it as dinner. Erin had wondered where all the catalogues on the dining-room table were going to go when people ate; the answer was, nowhere. There were two clear spots at the ends, where Aunt Joan and Uncle Druce usually sat; Aunt Joan moved a couple of piles so there was a third clear spot facing the living room, and told Erin that was her place. Uncle Druce leafed through a catalogue while he was eating; Aunt Joan read the paper. Erin looked over the piles of catalogues at the piano and thought about the toy boxes, which were still in the little room upstairs, because she'd been afraid that if she moved the broken knights a few at a time, they'd get scrambled and she'd never be able to fix them. So she'd put them carefully away, leaving out only the blue knight and his dog.

After they'd finished the main part of the meal, they

all took their plates to the kitchen, served themselves as much ice cream as they wanted, and came back to the table without a word. But after she'd finished her little scoop, Aunt Joan looked up from her paper and said, 'So, Erin. Did you find Sir Piers?'

Her voice was so unexpected in the midst of all that newspapery silence that Erin jumped. 'I'm sorry. Did I find who?'

'Sir Piers,' said Aunt Joan. 'He owns the castle in the toy boxes.'

Erin frowned. 'I thought the toy boxes belonged to kids in your family.'

'They did, literally speaking,' said Aunt Joan. 'But since our imaginations hadn't been suppressed by constant supervision, we believed that the castle in the toy boxes belonged to the most magnificent of the knights.'

Erin felt her mind freezing up, the way it did when she got something wrong. 'I see.' Then, suddenly, she did see. 'Oh! Is Sir Piers the one with the blue cloak?'

'Ah,' said Aunt Joan, with the expression that had crossed her face when she'd stroked the piano. 'So you *did* find him. Sir Piers the Peerless, we used to call him – the epitome of music and nobility, with his great deerhound Malachi, and all the knights in his retinue. We kids used to play with them for hours: battles, charges, sieges, bards singing of glorious deeds – the whole bit. Our father was as nuts about them as we were. He was a chivalry fanatic – he gave us quizzes on

The Boy's King Arthur at supper to be sure we were properly educated. How are they doing?'

She wouldn't have asked about them in that tone of voice if she'd known somebody had broken them. And if she'd really played with them, and really loved them, she'd be very upset if she knew. Then who knew what she'd say. 'Um . . . they're OK.'

'OK! I should say so! The oldest ones – Sir Piers and Malachi – are a hundred and fifty years old; four generations of children have collected the others and handed them on. Everybody's treasured them – and now, of course, they're irreplaceable.' Aunt Joan looked down at her paper. 'But I suppose they don't have much to say to the plastic-and-computer age . . . Never mind, dear. We'll put them in the attic.'

The attic! She was going to lose them! 'Oh, no! *Please* don't! They're wonderful! And Sir Piers is . . . is magnificent, like Sir Galahad or Sir Lancelot! It's just—!' She stopped, because she was afraid she'd cry if she went on.

'You like them? For heaven's sake, nobody could ever have guessed it from what you said. Well, of course we won't put them in the attic, then. But tell me something.' Aunt Joan's grey-green eyes looked at her quizzically. 'How have you, the kid who's having trouble in school, managed to read about Sir Galahad and Sir Lancelot?'

'I haven't. They're in a poem that's way above my level, but Rob had to study some of it in Honours

English, and he knew I liked pictures of knights and castles, so he read some of it to me. When he saw how much I liked it, he even read me some of the parts that weren't going to be on the test.'

'Very kind of him,' said Aunt Joan dryly.

There it was: an Aunt Joanism. You said something perfectly normal – nice, even – and you got a sarcastic answer. Erin finished her ice cream without looking up.

Aunt Joan picked up another section of her paper. 'No need to hang around, if you're finished. Bed at eight, your mother said, which isn't a bad idea. But so far as I'm concerned, you can read as late as you want—' Erin shook her head, but it didn't have any effect. 'Druce?'

Uncle Druce looked up from his catalogue with an absent smile.

'Erin likes *The Idylls of the King*. Where's Dad's special edition?'

'In the little room by the bathroom. The pile under the window.'

'Got that, Erin?' said Aunt Joan. 'It's really worth looking at – it has engravings by Gustave Doré, one of the very finest late-nineteenth-century illustrators, and he drew wonderful castles. You can take it into your room if you want. Just be sure to put it back exactly where it was when you're done, or it's gone for ever.'

Erin nodded, and when she got upstairs, she went to get the book; Aunt Joan might check, and anyway, she wanted to look at Sir Piers and Malachi again before she went to bed. They were standing right where she'd left them, in front of the book pile under the window, and neither of them laughed when the pile turned out to contain two books with 'King' in the title, and she had to hunt for illustrations inside them to decide which one Aunt Joan had meant. She'd meant the second one. It began with a picture of the sort of castle you dreamed of knights and ladies living in, on a cliff overlooking a river, with turrets and battlements and towers, all dark and mysterious. She took it to her room and got into her tights and Rob's tennis champion T-shirt, which was what she slept in, but the book was lying there so temptingly on the bed she decided she'd skim through the rest of its pictures before she brushed her teeth. Propping herself against the pillows, she opened it to the castle picture, then paged through to one of a king – Arthur, probably – on a splendid horse, looking down at two skeletons and a crown. Then a knight on a white horse, riding through a mysterious wood. The inside of a castle, with arches and tall windows, filled with men in tunics and ladies in beautiful long dresses . . .

When she woke up, the only light in the room came from the streetlight and the red dial of the digital electric clock next to her bed, which said 10:45. She watched the 5 slide into a 6, half her mind still in the wonderful castle she'd been building in her dreams. For a moment, she even thought she heard someone singing in that castle – then she realized she was drifting back to sleep and made herself get up to brush her teeth. She took her flashlight, but she didn't need it; Uncle Druce had gone to sleep over his bottle-cap sorting, so the light in his study was still on. She tiptoed by, used the bathroom as quietly as she could, and was just coming out when she heard Aunt Joan's door open. Quickly, she ducked into the room where the toy boxes were.

Aunt Joan's footsteps padded down the hall to the bathroom, paused, came in a step or two. Erin flattened herself against the wall, but Aunt Joan just closed the door, went into the bathroom, and ran water in the basin. It was like being shut into a closet; there were no streetlights on this side of the house, just the black wall of the house next door. Trembling, Erin switched on her flashlight and swung it slowly around the room, to remind herself how silly it was for an eleven-year-old to be afraid of the dark. There was the bed, the books, the toy boxes, the . . .

She stopped, blinking. The window had reflected her flashlight beam in a little circle, the way windows always did. But as she looked, the circle spread wider and wider, then began to change, the way the pictures in Rob's darkroom did when he developed them. At first, she could only see vague outlines, but gradually, they turned into towers and battlements – if it hadn't been for the window frame, she would have thought she was standing right next to them, looking down a parapet. Something blue flickered between two of the battlements; then slowly, slowly, a tall man with shoulder-length hair came into focus, his cloak billowing in the wind as he gazed over the walls. As she watched, he whistled, and a huge deerhound sprang out of a nearby tower door and loped up to him. The man patted it absently and looked back over the battlements. The dog started to lie down next to him, but then it turned towards Erin, sniffed the air, and looked at her.

Was it real? Could it see her? Was *she* real? Was she there?

The dog whined, and the man turned his head.

'What is it, Malachi?' His eyes followed the dog's gaze and swept over her, once, twice . . . The flashlight! She switched it off, but he scanned the window once more, his face probing, hesitant.

Behind Erin, the door swung open and a light blazed on. 'Good heavens!' said Aunt Joan's voice. 'What a turn you gave me, Erin! When I saw the light under the door, I thought a burglar had gotten in! What are you doing here at this hour?'

Erin blinked at the window in the bright light; there was nothing in it but the reflection of Aunt Joan, looking like an unmade bed with her hair down and her bathrobe untied. 'I . . . I don't know,' she said. 'I think I was asleep or something.'

'A sleepwalker,' said Aunt Joan, sighing. 'I might have known. Well, let's— Goodness! Sir Piers and Malachi

30

in *here*? I thought the toy boxes were in your room!'

'Oh,' said Erin, blushing. 'I told the men to go left instead of right.'

'You mean, right instead of left,' said Aunt Joan, smiling. 'And of course they're too heavy for a child to lift, so you couldn't fix it. Well, no harm done; they're probably better off in here anyway. Come on, dear – let's get you back to bed.'

She put a hand on Erin's shoulder and guided her towards the door. Erin looked back quickly as the light snapped off, but the window had gone completely dark.

3
Faking

When she thought about it in the morning, Erin decided maybe she had been sleepwalking. She'd done that − not often enough to worry about, the doctor said, but a couple of times − and what with the toy boxes and the illustrations, she'd had castles on the brain, as Rob would say. What's more, since she'd been dreaming about castles, it wouldn't be all that surprising for her to sleepwalk to where one was. Except she hadn't *felt* asleep. She'd brushed her teeth and everything. And every time she thought about it, she could still feel Sir Piers's eyes look for her, as if she had almost been in his world, but not quite.

She puzzled it over and over, which she had had lots of time to do, because nobody in this house knew what structured time was. Uncle Druce sorted bottle caps during breakfast, then put on a green cloth jacket with JOE'S PARKING GARAGE on the back and left for work; Aunt Joan drank more coffee and read the morning paper. That was all that had happened by 9:00, and it looked as if the next action was going to be lunch.

Maybe, just maybe, there was something funny about the window. The rain had stopped, so she went out into the back yard to look, but all that got her was wet feet. The last upstairs window on the side, which was the one it had to be, looked just like the others – big, with wavy old glass covered by a screen. She sighed, slapped the mosquito that was settling on her arm, and glanced around the yard. Except that everything was alive, it looked as shabby as the rest of the house. The wisteria that grew over the back of the house was so thick they'd had to trim it so they could get out the door, and the honeysuckle sprawled all over the fence. What was supposed to be a lawn was filled with purple and white violets, so the grass had moved in with the irises and other flowers that were trying to bloom in what had once been a garden. Too bad – it would be really pretty if someone took care of it, but obviously, they didn't care about gardens any more than they cared about furniture. Well, she'd better go fix those knights.

Inside the back door, she pulled the grass out of her sandals and dried her feet, trying to think how to ask for glue without explaining why she needed it. But she might as well have saved herself the effort; Aunt Joan was gone, the funny way people came and went in this house without telling anybody. Both the dining room and the living room were empty — except, of course, for the old furniture, the bottle caps and the piano.

The piano. And nobody was around.

She walked to it, tilted back the keyboard cover and gazed at the keys, wondering if she dared to play. There were no earphones, no volume control, and the piano was so big, you'd be able to hear it all over the house, maybe even across the street. She looked out the window at the big trees and shabby houses. There was no guessing how many people you'd disturb if you played. And when you made a mistake, everybody would know.

But there was the piano, shining, perfect . . . silent. Gently, she touched its golden label, then stroked a couple of the keys. They weren't plastic; they were yellower, and they felt very different. She pressed one. The note was a little out of tune, but the way the key felt when you pushed it down was really nifty. She pushed another key down, then another, half expect-ing Aunt Joan to come stop her. But nothing happened.

Hesitantly, she sat down and played one of the sad little pieces she'd liked when she'd taken lessons. It was different out of tune, but you could sort of correct that in your head, and the sound was amazing. Rich. Warm. Huge. She finished the piece and thought a minute. There'd been another one that had sounded like bells. It had been kind of disappointing at home, but on this piano . . . She scooted herself forward on the bench so she could reach the pedal and started. Ding-dong, ding-dong, BELL, BELL. The sound boomed out of the piano, asking her to play louder. DING-DONG, DING-DONG, *BELL, BELL*. Oh, wow. She stopped, looking over her shoulder, then out the window, but nobody was listening. She started again, and this time she went on into the part with chords, the hairs on the back of her neck prickling with excitement as she came to the passage with the huge BONGs in the bass. It took three times through to play it without mistakes, but the third time sounded great, and by then, other pieces had turned up in her mind. It had been over a year since she'd played them, but her fingers seemed to remember where to go, and as she played, things came into her head she hadn't thought of for ages. Silly things, like the new sofa that had come when she'd been practising this piece, or the place Mom had taken her for tests when she'd been practising this one . . . her fingers stumbled. How did it go? She tried to fix it, but she was stuck. Maybe she should stop, anyway. She'd been playing quite a while. She slid off the bench, started towards the door, and stopped, her heart thumping.

Aunt Joan was sitting at the dining-room table, watching her.

'Good heavens, dear,' she said. 'Don't look so guilty! It's no crime to play the piano. Why did you say you didn't?'

'I'm sorry. I thought you meant lessons.'

'You quit? That's a real shame.'

'Yeah, but . . . well . . . there was a problem, and Mom and Dad felt it would be better for me to concentrate on my schoolwork.'

Anybody else would have left it there, but Aunt Joan wasn't anybody else. 'What kind of problem could possibly have convinced your parents you should quit?'

'I . . . um . . . I'd been faking. And the psychologist told Mom I had to stop doing that or I'd never—'

'How do you fake playing the piano?'

'You look at the music as if you can read it, when you can't.'

Aunt Joan should have looked shocked, the way everybody else had when the faking business had come out, but instead she looked interested. 'How did you learn those pieces if you can't read music?'

It was a real question, not the kind that was designed to put you on the spot, but Erin gulped just the same. Up until now, nobody had asked it. That had been lucky, because the answer was Rob, who'd played her pieces when she'd 'accidentally' left them on the piano; that way, he'd said, she could get the tune into her ear so the notes on the page would mean something. The notes never had, but once she'd heard the pieces a couple of times, she could figure them out, and that had seemed just as good. At least, it had until the psychologist had explained that that sort of thing was faking, and said it was wrong. Rob had said it *wasn't* just faking, it really *helped*, and he'd wanted to tell

Mom and Dad how he'd been playing her pieces and reading her homework stories to her – but she'd made him absolutely, totally promise not to. It was bad enough for her to disgrace everybody by faking; she didn't even dare think how much worse it would've been if Rob told them he'd been in on it. Of course she'd never squeal on him, but Aunt Joan was pretty sharp. She might keep asking. 'Um,' she said, 'I need to go to the bathroom.'

Aunt Joan smiled. 'Well, that's allowed,' she said. 'And since you're going up there, bring down the Tennyson you were looking at last night, and let's read it together.'

Oh, boy. A reading session. Erin nodded and climbed the stairs, her stomach churning so hard she spent a little extra time in the bathroom, waiting to throw up. But the dizziness and sweating didn't lead to anything this time, so she fetched the beautiful book from her room and took it back down.

Aunt Joan opened the book to the picture of the castle and the pale lady on the barge in the river below it. 'It really is a wonderful engraving, isn't it?' she said. 'Everything a castle should be, and below it, beautiful Elaine, who died for love of Sir Lancelot, poor child.' She turned to the first page. 'Let's find out how it happened.'

So it was a story about Elaine! Erin clutched at the hint. Yes, the word in funny type at the top of the page started with what might be an E. 'Elaine,' she read, then looked at Aunt Joan. 'That's the title, right?'

Aunt Joan nodded. 'Go on.'

Erin put a shaky finger on the first line to keep it steady, and stared at the first word. It began with an E, too, and though it was in a different kind of type, it looked enough like the title word to be the same. As for the rest of it – she slid her finger along under the words. 'Elaine the far, Elaine the live, Elaine the little man of . . . of Austria, high in the chair up a town in the eats, guard dog the saccharine shell of Ladyship—'

'Erin,' Aunt Joan broke in gently, 'can you tell me what that means?'

Erin stared at the page as if she were studying it, but as usual it didn't do any good. She swallowed down the vomity taste in her mouth and shook her head.

'Well, to be fair, I can't tell what it means, either,' said Aunt Joan. 'It doesn't have much to do with what's on the page. Listen:

> 'Elaine the fair, Elaine the loveable,
> Elaine, the lily maid of Astolat,
> High in her chamber up a tower to the east
> Guarded the sacred shield of Lancelot.'

She looked up. 'Can you tell me what *that* means?'

'It means that Elaine was beautiful and really sweet; and she was sitting in the east tower of Astolat Castle, guarding Sir Lancelot's shield.'

'Very good,' said Aunt Joan. 'Try reading it again, now.'

'I . . . I'm not supposed to do that. Ever.'

'Ever? Why not?'

'Because when I know what it says, I'm not really reading; I'm just pointing to the words and saying what I know they have to be, so people *think* I'm getting the words off the page instead of out of my head. That's faking, and it's . . . deceitful.'

'Deceitful! Good heavens! You've never been a deceitful child.'

'I didn't mean to be . . . I used to think everybody read that way, only they were smarter . . . later I realized that was wrong, but I didn't know how to change . . .'

Aunt Joan snorted. 'You'd think the fancy school you go to would have picked it up in first grade – second at the latest.'

'That's what the psychologist said when he looked at my test scores, but it really wasn't the school's fault. They did notice, but everybody could see how scared I got on those tests, so they believed Mom when she said she'd been like that and had outgrown it. And I was good in class – at least until this year. Even the psychologist admitted that; after we'd talked a while, he said I'd made a fine art of something-or-other deceit.'

'Compensatory,' muttered Aunt Joan. Then her eyebrows shot up. 'Oh – *that's* why you thought you'd been deceitful!'

'Using a fancy word for faking doesn't make it right.'

'I see,' said Aunt Joan thoughtfully. 'And it's wrong to fake when you play the piano, too?'

'Faking's always wrong.'

Aunt Joan's eyebrows rose. 'Some people call it playing by ear. Do you know what that means?'

Erin thought a minute. 'It means . . . not having a plan. Just sort of bumbling along and seeing what happens.'

'Well, yes, it does,' said Aunt Joan. 'And I suppose that's bad?'

Erin looked down. 'Mom says kids like me need structure.'

'I know she does,' said Aunt Joan grimly. 'Well, we've had our structure for this morning. You're free, now.'

Erin picked up the book and zipped upstairs so fast she'd gotten all the way to her room before she remembered she'd forgotten to ask for the glue. If she went down again, Aunt Joan might say more nasty things about Mom, so she disappeared into the window seat until she saw Uncle Druce shamble around the corner and down the street. She checked her watch: 12:20. She'd better get ready for lunch.

She washed her face, because she'd been crying a little about the reading and missing Mom and Dad and especially Rob, and went downstairs. The dining room was empty, but Aunt Joan's voice floated in from the kitchen.

'. . . Serious enough. She can't hear a word she reads. But the real problem is that they've handled it true to the Family pattern: years of denial, and now a guilt trip. Poor kid. Not a *single attempt* to teach her how to compensate in her own way, would you believe? In fact, everyone she's worked with seems to have *stopped* her from compensating and insisted that she learn *their* way. No wonder the school insisted on the camp; that's the only way they could help her . . . tea or coffee?'

'Tea,' said Uncle Druce, and came out the kitchen door, carrying two plates.

Aunt Joan raised her voice. 'You should hear her on the piano. You'd never expect it from a little mouse like her, but she plays with real authority. What an ear!' The refrigerator door slammed shut. 'And they made her *quit*!'

Uncle Druce put one plate at Erin's place and one at his own, glanced at the doorway where she was standing, then sat down and began on his sandwich. Erin stood still, her face flaming scarlet. Luckily, she was more or less the right colour again by the time Aunt Joan stumped in with the third sandwich and the teapot, so she could walk in as if she'd just gotten there. Uncle Druce could have called her on it, but he just threw her a sideways look and went on eating. As she bit gratefully into her own sandwich, it occurred to her that if she wanted glue without questions, he was the one to ask. It might be worth a try, anyway.

She got the chance to try it sooner than she'd thought, because Aunt Joan went out after lunch, and instead of going back to work, Uncle Druce went up to his study. Quickly, Erin hurried to the little room and opened the toy chest with the knights in it. She'd found out yesterday there was a head for each knight in the casualty ward; all she had to do was try one head around until she found a fit. It took a while, but she finally got one she was sure was right. Taking a deep breath, she took it down the hall and knocked on the jamb by Uncle Druce's door.

Uncle Druce looked up from his bottle caps, his face so surprised that she almost slipped away, but she thought of Sir Piers and held her ground. 'Um, could you tell me where I could find some glue?'

He pointed to his desk, but the glue there was the kind you used on paper.

'I don't think that will do. I need the kind you use on model airplanes or broken plates. In two tubes, that you mix.'

'Epoxy,' he said. 'It's a bit tricky to use. You sure the other stuff won't do?'

'I don't think so. It's got to hold a knight together.'

He looked up sharply, and suddenly she realized she'd given herself away. What an idiot she was! Nobody knew the knights were broken but her. Which meant if he found out, he might accuse *her* of breaking them, and there would be nobody to back her up . . . ! But all he said was, 'Broken, huh? You got it there? Let me take a look.'

She stepped across the room and gave him the

knight and the head. He turned them over in his hand, then gave them back. 'Epoxy won't do it,' he said. 'It needs to be soldered, and I don't have a soldering iron.'

'Then they – then he can't be fixed?' she said, trying to keep her voice steady.

He shook his head and went back to his sorting. She crept back to the little room and put the broken knight into the casualty ward. 'I'm sorry,' she said to him – to all of them. 'I'll keep trying.'

No, that was faking. She *couldn't* keep trying; she didn't know what a soldering iron was. And she was so stupid – stupid, dumb, dim-witted! – she couldn't do what any other fifth grader would do, which was look it up. People had tried to help her not be dumb, but each one of them – teachers, the psychologist, Mom's friends, and now, Aunt Joan – said what all the *other* people had suggested was wrong. What was really wrong, of course, was her. If she could only disappear, fade away, never be wrong again . . . !

She picked up Sir Piers and Malachi, wrapped them in tissue paper, and put them gently back into the toy box. Then she tiptoed back to the window seat in her room.

4
A Song in the Castle

There *wasn't* anybody singing. Erin gave her pillow a despairing thump and turned over for the millionth time. She'd listened and listened, even stuck her head out the window and looked up and down the street – not a sound, unless you counted a car now and then. It was her imagination keeping her awake again. When that happened at home, Mom fixed her a cup of camomile tea, but nobody believed in herbs in this house – you didn't even have to ask – and anyway, Aunt Joan and Uncle Druce had gone to bed. She locked her hands behind her head and looked at the moonbeam that stretched across the room like a wall. A castle wall, like the one in her sleepwalking dream last night. If she had been sleepwalking. If it had been a . . . *There it was again.*

She slipped out of bed, hardly daring to breathe. It was so far away she couldn't hear any words, but it was definitely a song. Not out on the street; somewhere behind the house. Outside one of the back windows . . . like the window with a castle in it. No, that was impossible. Silly. Crazy. OK, but suppose she went and checked, just to see . . .

Sure. And suppose Aunt Joan found her there again.

Yeah, but if she got her towel out of the bathroom and stuffed it under the door, nobody would know she was in there, unless she made noise. Which she wouldn't.

She tiptoed down the hall, stopping every time a board creaked. Aunt Joan's door was closed. Uncle Druce's was open, but he was snoring. Quickly, she slipped into the toy-box room, closed its door, and bent down to stuff the towel under it.

Behind her, something clanked.

She whirled round, fumbling with the switch on her flashlight, but the room was getting brighter all by itself. Above the toy boxes, the window slowly developed into the castle parapet she'd seen last night, and the clanking got louder. Gradually, three knights came into focus, pointing over the battlements as they walked. They were moving away from her; that meant they were coming from someplace in the castle she couldn't see. Was it like a TV, or if she got closer to the window, could she see more? Stepping carefully around the toy boxes, she put one hand on the window frame.

It wasn't like TV. There was real wind on her face, smelling of country things, and though there wasn't any singing, there was plenty of shouting, mixed with sounds of hammering and the clatter of horses' feet. She looked back, clutching the frame. There was the little room, with the toy boxes, the books and the closed door. In front of her was the parapet, wide enough for ten knights to walk on side by side, and so high all she could see over the battlements was the sky. Gingerly, she tapped the stones beyond the window frame with one foot, half expecting the castle to dissolve like a dream. But it didn't; it was absolutely solid. And immense. Beyond the towers on each side of her, the walls stretched back to other towers in a rectangle so enormous she could hardly see it all. Inside those walls, there was – what?

She tiptoed to the inside wall and looked over, her eyes widening. Diagonally across from her, a long row of pointed arches supported tall windows that over-looked a courtyard the size of a city block, and just as busy. On the wall opposite the arcade were one hundred stalls, and in front of them, scores of stable-boys were grooming and saddling big, muscular horses. Near them, squires were buckling knights into knee-length tunics of chain mail, and pages were shining shields or oiling lances. Beyond them, in front of a low building that jutted out from the wall where the stalls ended, two boys in brown were pumping a huge bellows at a fire, and a man in a leather apron pulled a glowing piece of metal out of the coals, lifted it onto his anvil and pounded it with ringing strokes.

Suddenly, one of the dogs who had been lounging in the sun scrambled to its feet and barked; a minute later, a group of riders swirled through the gates in a wave of brightly coloured cloaks, and pages in blue hurried towards them. Amidst the flurry of dismounting, shouts and steaming horses, a baritone voice floated upward on a chance breeze. Not an ordinary voice – a wonderful voice, rich and full and sad.

> *'Western wind, when wilt thou blow*
> *That the small rain down can rain . . .'*

That must have been what she'd heard in her room! And it was coming from . . . She turned round slowly, listening as the voice finished the song. It was coming from the tower with the banner on it. If she went down, maybe she could see who it was.

She looked over her shoulder; all she could see of the window was its faint outline against the battlements, but as she walked towards it, it was as clearly visible as it had been before. It was there, then; all she had to do was count the number of battlements between it and the tower so she could find it again, and she could sneak down just for a minute. One, two, three . . . She sidled down the wall, looking around anxiously. Eight, nine . . .

The door to the tower burst open, and a guard marched out, armed with a pike and a short sword. There was absolutely no place to hide; and the window was too far away to run to. Erin backed against the wall, praying he'd turn the other way, but he marched straight towards her – and past her, to the other tower. He swung open its door and went in; a minute later, he appeared at the top, his pike glimmering in the sun. She turned and looked at the tower closer to her. There was a guard up there, too, looking down right into her eyes. But nothing happened; his gaze swept over her and along the walls.

She stretched out a hand and looked at it. She could see *herself* OK. Was it just a dream, then? Or . . . or was it possible that she'd really disappeared, the way she'd always wanted to? If she had, she could go anywhere in the castle she wanted; all she'd have to do was stay quiet and out of the way. Maybe. With a shiver, she remembered the way Sir Piers had *almost* seen her last night. Well, she'd be very careful.

She hurried to the tower and yanked open its heavy door. Inside, stairs spiralled up and down, so narrow and so worn by hundreds of feet that she kept one hand on the wall as she started down. The wall was interrupted every couple of spirals by little arches that led to funny-shaped rooms in the tower. They would make great places to hide if she met somebody, so she stopped, listening, at every one. But the only sounds came from the courtyard – the blacksmith's hammer, the clatter of horses' hooves, then suddenly a shout of 'Halt!' What could it be? She peered out the next narrow window that overlooked the courtyard, just in time to see two guards raise the axes they had crossed in the gateway. As everyone watched, a squire dressed all in crimson trotted into the courtyard and pulled up his handsome charger. A group of knights clustered around him, some of them with their hands on their sword hilts, but after he'd spoken a few words to them, a couple of them clapped him on the back, and the others called pages to put up his horse.

She would have stood there watching, but the voice started to sing again. Now it was close, just a little way below her. Slowly, she crept down the stairs, drawn by the sound. After two more spirals she reached an arch that opened into a high vaulted room hung with tapestries on one side and lit by arched windows on the other. In its centre was a table covered with all sorts of musical instruments, and sitting on its far side, with Malachi at his feet, was Sir Piers.

She hadn't made any noise she could think of, but he broke off in the middle of a bar and glanced up. Had he seen her? Sensed her? She ducked back behind the heavy open door. After a few seconds, he tuned his instrument and began again. The song was different from any song she'd ever heard; it told a story – a sad one about a dead knight and three ravens – and its tune was very simple. But his voice made it magical, and what he did with his instrument wasn't at all like the accompaniment that came off pages of music at school or church. It was more like embroidery, a melody of its own that wandered around his voice.

Creeping forward, she watched his fingers fly over the strings.

Behind her, footsteps raced up the stairs. She slipped quickly out the doorway — and almost crashed into the page who was hurrying towards it. He hesitated, looking around, and she got ready to run, but he brushed right past her and paused a few feet inside the room. It hadn't just been the guards, then. She had disappeared. She peered around the open door. Across the room, Malachi got up, and Sir Piers stopped halfway through a verse. Neither of them looked pleased at the interruption, but Sir Piers smiled wearily.

'Your face tells me you have brought urgent news, William,' he said. 'Come, tell me what it is.'

William blushed, looked around uneasily, then pulled himself together. 'A squire has just come from Sir Roger of Woodstock, seeking your patronage in his name.'

'That is impossible,' said Sir Piers gently. 'Sir Roger of Woodstock was a gallant knight and a true friend, but as he met his death a year ago, he can send no squires now.'

'I crave your pardon,' said William. 'I was . . . unclear. I didn't mean to say that Sir Roger of Woodstock sent the squire. He is here in his own name: Giles, Sir Roger's son.'

Sir Piers got up slowly. 'Giles!' he said, smiling. 'I have not seen him since he was a child. How quickly time passes, that he is of an age to need patronage now

. . . but how sorely he must need it, without his father. Assure him of my welcome, and send him here as soon as he's bathed and rested.'

William bowed and turned to go, but Sir Piers suddenly held up a hand. 'Wait!' As the boy looked back in surprise, Sir Piers pointed at Malachi.

Ever since the dog had followed Sir Piers to the table, he'd been looking towards the door, sniffing the air; now he took a few steps forward, his lips curling.

'Malachi!' called Sir Piers. As William stepped uneasily to the side, he added, 'He's not snarling at you; he sees something else.' He laid his hand on the dog's head as he returned to him, and both their eyes searched the doorway.

William scanned it, too, his face perplexed. 'I don't see anything,' he said. 'But as I was coming in, I felt — I'm not sure what.' He glanced up ruefully at Sir Piers. 'It was that that made me confuse my message.'

Sir Piers looked down as Malachi shoved his nose into his hand. This time, when the dog started forward, Sir Piers went with him, and William followed, drawing his dagger.

Seizing the side of the door, Erin shoved it shut and dashed towards the steps. It wouldn't do much good, of course; they'd let Malachi out when they opened it, and there was no way she could run faster than a deerhound. But it was pretty dark in the tower; if she could get a head start, maybe they'd go down instead of up . . .

Except the stairway didn't go down. It only went up – and not in a stone spiral. Peering through the murky light, she saw an ordinary wood staircase running steeply up between two plaster walls. Frantically, she looked one way, the other, then quickly behind her, expecting to see Malachi leap out the door. The door wasn't the one she'd shut; it was half the size, it wasn't arched. And it was in a different place.

She put her hand on the wall, swallowing back the vomity taste of panic. Lost. Or 'disoriented', if you wanted the politer word the psychologist used for it. Just the dumb sort of thing she'd do. *Other* people didn't get mixed up when a place looked different going one way than it did going the other, but she was so hopelessly, totally stupid . . .

OK, but what was really hopelessly, totally stupid was standing here, instead of running up the stairs there were. *Somewhere* at the top of them was the window back to Aunt Joan's, and if she couldn't find it fast, there'd be trouble. She tiptoed up the narrow steps, swallowing harder and harder as it grew lighter. Because there was no door at the top. There were no stones, no battlements. There was just the inside of a peaked roof, slanting down to a wall lined with old skis, sleds, trunks, suitcases . . . and shimmering so vaguely against the unfinished wood that she could hardly see it, something dark and shiny, like maybe a mirror, or . . .

Reaching the top of the stairs, she took a step closer,

hardly daring to hope. Yes, it was a window. And on its sill, barely visible through the reflection of the room around her, was a yellow flashlight. With a little squeak of relief, she started towards it – then stopped dead. Behind her own reflected image, she saw another one jump to its feet. Whirling round, she saw a boy with a pale face and a thatch of cowlicky hair.

5
A Con Man

With a gasp, she reached for the window frame. She was probably safe, being disappeared and all, but he'd obviously sensed something, and the faster she got out of here, the—

'Hey!' said the boy. 'Take it easy!'

He'd seen her! Erin turned back, staring.

The boy's half-friendly brown eyes met hers. 'You *sure* you want to jump? You'll be OK, I suppose. There's a thousand-gallon vat of Roquefort dressing out there, carefully placed to save people who sneak up on me, only to discover I'm an ogre. But you might want to consider what a mess landing will be.'

Looking behind her, she saw what he saw – not *her* window, which was still flickering against the attic walls, but a smaller window next to it that looked out over a lawn three floors down. He couldn't see her way out, then. Weird, but lucky.

'Don't worry, I won't jump,' she said. 'But if

you'll close your eyes a minute, I'll go away. Promise.'

'That's not as good an idea as it sounds,' he said. 'See, when you get downstairs, your mom and my mom will bring you right back; then we'll both get a lecture on the importance of being polite to mothers' friends' children. Generally, it's wiser to accept these little social burdens gracefully.'

So he thought she was one of those bratty kids you had to entertain when their moms visited your mom, just when you'd hoped to have a little disappearing time. Great. That meant she didn't have to explain. But the poor guy! She looked around the attic. Nails from the roof shingles coming through the unfinished ceilings. Bare light bulbs. An old-fashioned record player, a tattered couch, big wooden boxes and a rack of period clothes. It was the perfect place to disappear.

'I'm sorry I bothered you,' she said. 'I didn't mean to come here. In fact, I don't even know where "here" is. So if you'll—'

'You don't know where "here" is!' he said, slapping his forehead with his palm. 'Of course! I should have guessed! You've got the wrong address. The psychiatrist's office is three houses down the road; he has special sessions for people who don't know where they are. The only problem is getting the people to the sessions.'

'I'm *not* a psycho, I'm—'

'—just a little confused. Sure. What's your name?'

'Erin Westford. But look—'

'Error,' he said, smiling. 'How fitting.'

'I said Erin!'

'Anything you say. My name's Con, as in con man. When I'm not busy being an ogre, I specialize in dumb riddles and word games. As for example, Why did the moron buy a truckload of Cheerios?'

She used the time she was supposed to be thinking of an answer to glance at her window. It was still there. Maybe she should just humour him until he turned his back. Of course, it would blow him out of the water when he found her gone, which was too bad, because you could see he was trying to be nice, but—

'Well?' he said.

'Tell me – I can hardly stand the suspense.'

'Because he thought they were doughnut seeds!' He grinned as she giggled. 'That's more like it. Let's try another: A big moron and a little moron were standing next to a cliff. The big moron fell off and died; but the little one didn't. Why not?'

'Because he landed in a thousand-gallon vat of Roquefort dressing?'

'Technically, no; the answer is: Because he was a little more on. But your answer isn't bad. There's hope for you.'

'Gee, thanks.' Trouble was, if this went on too long, she'd never get back to Aunt Joan's. The best thing to do, probably, was to distract him. She pointed from the old skis to the record player. 'You specialize in antiques as well as riddles?'

'Antiques!' he said indignantly. 'This is so new you don't even know what it is! It's called a stereo, short for stereophonic sound – like three-D for recorded music. I won't confuse you with the details, but it has two speakers. Listen.'

He took a record out of a cardboard case, set it on an old-fashioned turntable, and slowly lowered the needle onto it. Between the way he did it – like it was an everyday thing – and what he'd said about two speakers . . . she looked at him as the scratches and clicks turned into the slightly canned sound of an orchestra and a piano, playing huge, splashy chords. T-shirt with no logo. Pants, not jeans, and no logo on them either. Leather shoes and white socks (gross!). And except for the cowlicks, his hair was greased back, like in the days of Elvis. The question wasn't just *where* she was, but *when*.

'Fantastic, huh?' he asked. 'Van Cliburn right in your own attic.' He looked at her quizzically. 'You've heard of him, right? The pianist who just won the Tchaikovsky competition in Moscow?'

No way was she going to admit she hadn't. 'Oh,' she said. 'Him.'

'*Oh, him*,' mimicked Con. 'Just the world's coolest pianist, playing what he's made the world's most famous concerto. You know this piece, right?'

'I've heard it—' which she had: it turned up sometimes when Rob tuned into the Top 100 Classics to study by – 'But that's different from knowing who wrote it or what it is.'

57

'Boy,' he said. 'I don't know about you. Sure, some-times I have to think a bit before I remember who wrote a piece I'm playing, but when I play this—'

Erin's eyes opened wide. 'You can play *this*? Like, on the piano?'

'What else would I play it on?'

'A radio? A harmonica? I mean—' she jerked her head towards the record as the pianist roared up and down the keyboard – 'I mean, listen to him. You've got to be an awesome pianist to play that.'

'An awesome pianist,' he muttered. 'Hey, that's cool.'

'Then it's the harmonica or bust?'

'OK, OK,' he said defensively, 'so I have to fake some parts. But that's only because I haven't practised it. There's this big concerto contest coming up, and I'm working on a Mozart – easier technically, but lots harder musically, because . . . well, it's hard to explain to somebody who doesn't play.'

'But I do play. Some, anyway.'

'You *do*?' Con's face lit up. 'What are you working on?'

'Um, little pieces by Bach, and Schumann, Bartók, and . . .' his look made her go on with Rob's pieces, which she could sort of play . . . 'sonatinas by Clementi and Haydn.'

'The usual,' he said, shrugging. 'Can you improvise?'

'Can I what?'

'You know, take a piece like "Three Blind Mice" and make it sound like Tchaikovsky—' he nodded at the record player – 'or like a Bach fugue, or like jazz.'

She stared at him. 'You can *do* that?'

'Well,' he said, '*I* can do it. *Other* people can do it. So it can be done. But not by little girls who just stick to the music on the page.' He threw her a patronizing look. 'Little Error plays the piano so *sweetly* for Mommy and Daddy's guests . . .'

Erin turned towards her window. 'Pardon me. I'm leaving.'

'Heck, I'm sorry.' And he really looked sorry. 'All I meant was, *real* pianists don't just take lessons, you know? They like it. They play by ear.'

'I *do* like it! And I play by ear all the time!'

'All *right*,' he said enthusiastically. 'Well, heck, if you can do that, all you need to do is listen to lots of music – all kinds. And you get the way each kind of music sounds into your head, and when you improvise, you make what you've memorized sound like that.' He sighed as he looked at her puzzled face. 'I could show you in a second if the piano were up here. Talking about music never works; you need a demonstration. My dad was a *great* improviser. He's dead now, but he taught me everything until I was ten. Then . . .' His face clouded. 'Well, then I went on to other teachers, and they said I was a prodigy.'

'For real?'

'Yeah,' he said modestly, 'but I try not to let it turn my head. I may have to settle for just being an awesome pianist. But you never know. I told you I was playing in a competition, right? Well, I'm only in seventh grade, and all the other people playing are seniors in high—'

Somewhere below them, a door opened. 'Con?' called a woman's voice. 'What are you doing up there? I *told* you we were going at three!'

Con made a face and took the needle off the record, which was still playing. 'Right there,' he said. 'I just thought, since you had guests—'

'Guests?'

Uh-oh. Erin turned towards her window. It had faded a little, but as she edged towards it, it got clearer. If Con would just turn away . . .!

But he didn't turn away; he looked at her really carefully, and held up a finger. 'OK, Mom,' he said loudly. 'Just let me get my shoes on, and I'll be down.'

'Hurry up!' she said. And the door closed.

Con's face went completely serious, for once. 'Um,' he said. 'I've got to go, obviously. Wait till we drive off, then you can just walk down the stairs and leave. Nobody'll see you, and I won't tell anybody you came.'

'OK,' she said. 'Thanks.'

'Think nothing of it,' he said, waving his hand airily. 'Just so you come back.'

'Um . . . it's complicated.'

'I bet it is. Life's tough for people who don't know where they are. But remember, it's only three houses down from where you want to be. And I could teach you to improvise.' A car crunched on the gravel drive outside the house, and a horn blew twice. 'Give it a whirl,' he said, and raced down the stairs.

She waited until she heard the door at the bottom close behind him; then she moved towards the window and picked up her flashlight. Stepping on the sill, she flicked on the beam and ran it around the little room at Aunt Joan's. Everything was exactly the same: the toy boxes, the books, the towel stuffed under the door. No castle. Well, of course. She was standing in the window where the castle had been.

Behind and below her, a door slammed and a car started to drive away — but the sound stopped dead as she stepped across the sill and jumped down, and when she looked back, the window was just a window.

6
Patterns

Breakfast was exactly like yesterday's breakfast, except there was wholewheat toast instead of white. Uncle Druce ate three pieces with peanut butter and grape jelly; Aunt Joan ate one piece with no butter and a little marmalade. Thinking in a lonely sort of way about breakfast at home, with oatmeal and yoghurt, fresh fruit and orange juice, Erin decided to live dangerously and have grape jelly on one piece and marmalade on the other. Not very exciting either way. What she really wanted was to go back to bed and sleep for a couple more hours. Well, after Uncle Druce left . . .

But as the front door closed behind Uncle Druce, Aunt Joan pulled something out from under the sections of the newspaper she hadn't gotten to yet. 'Erin, I want you to look at this.'

Oh, no. She should have skipped the toast altogether; what she was supposed to look at was a

reading workbook. Not the usual kind, with one of
those fake cheerful covers that tried to convince you
reading was fun, fun, fun! Its cover sheet was blue, with
no graphics at all, but as soon as Aunt Joan flipped that
back (which she had to, because it was stapled together
in one corner) anybody could tell what it was.

'All right,' said Aunt Joan. 'What I need you to do
is— Erin? Are you all right?'

Erin swallowed hard. 'Sure.'

Aunt Joan didn't look like she believed that, but she
didn't stop. 'OK,' she said, taking away Erin's plate and
plopping the workbook down where it had been.
'What you need to do is look at this and tell me . . .'
Her voice went on, and Erin looked down obediently
at the page, pushing her hair behind her ears. Not that
it helped; the buzzing that always drowned out instructions came from inside the ears, not outside.

a
m k
m x w
p z m v
r m n q s
h p r w v s
m p q y x q c
c n q p m z x w
w p r m w q v z q

What was she supposed to do? It was so hard to

understand things when there were all those terrible words staring at you. She looked up, but instead of a helpful teacher, there was only Aunt Joan, frowning. Well, she'd just have to try. 'A make mix prize—'

Aunt Joan's newspaper landed on the workbook with a thump, and Aunt Joan's voice said, 'Well, I can see why that psychologist of yours said you had to stop faking.'

'I wasn't . . . !' The words died away, and the lie with them. Erin cringed, waiting for all the awful things Aunt Joan was going to say, but all Aunt Joan did was pour herself more coffee and take a sip.

'Let's try again,' she said, putting down her cup. 'This time, I'm going to tell you what I want you to do *before* I take the newspaper off that page. But in order to tell you what to do, I need to know what you saw when you looked at it. Tell me.'

'Um . . .' This was awful. 'Words.'

'You *saw* words?'

'Well, I saw letters. And letters make words.'

'Do letters *always* make words? Can they make other things? Like patterns?'

'I guess so.'

'OK. Do you remember if the letters on that page made a pattern?'

'Oh! You mean, that triangle?'

For once she'd said the right thing; Aunt Joan smiled. 'So you did see a triangle!'

'Sure. I just didn't think it counted.'

'In this house,' said Aunt Joan tartly, 'what you see *always* counts.'

Always? Even if it was a castle in a windowpane that turned into an attic? Of course, you could split hairs (if you were Rob's sister, you got good at that) and say that the windowpane wasn't *in* the house. Or the attic, either, for that matter – there'd been time to check that out before breakfast, and the attic in this house was just a crawl space filled with suitcases and boxes of papers. And if the castle and the attic weren't really in the house, of course seeing them *didn't* count . . .

Aunt Joan tapped her hand – none too gently. 'So tell me once more. What did you see on that page?'

Erin jumped, feeling her face go red. 'Um . . . a triangle of words . . . No, wait! A triangle of letters.'

'Good,' said Aunt Joan. She took the newspaper off the page and pointed to the triangle. 'See how the letters are in rows? What I want you to do is look at the letters in one row at a time, starting at the top. How many letters are there in the first row?'

There had to be some catch. It couldn't be this simple. 'One.'

'And in the second?'

'Two.'

'Good. And three in the third, and four in the fourth – never mind counting them; that's not what we're here for. What I want you to do is look at each line – the whole line. After a few lines, you'll have to move your eyes back and forth to see all the letters; when you have to do that, put your finger on the line where it happens.'

Erin stared at it. The first line was a snap; the second, no problem. The third, OK; the fourth . . . hmm. She blinked, tried again, and looked up at Aunt Joan. 'Um, how many letters *should* I be able to see all at once?'

'We're not talking about what you *should* be seeing,' said Aunt Joan. 'We're talking about what you *do* see. For sure. Before it wobbles and you can't quite tell.'

It wobbled for other people, too? Well, then. 'Three, for sure. It wobbles at four.'

'Excellent,' said Aunt Joan.

'It *is*?'

'Absolutely. It means you can read three-letter words without faking – if you can bring yourself to believe what you see.'

'Three-letter words! That's *first grade*!'

Aunt Joan shrugged. 'First-grade words don't disappear when you go into second. Take this newspaper, for instance.' She flipped it back to the first page. 'Look over the headlines – all the ones bigger than the regular print – and tell me how many words there are with three letters or fewer.'

A newspaper! There was no way she could—!

'I'm not asking you to *read* it,' said Aunt Joan, as if she'd read her mind. 'I'm just asking you to *see* it. And as for those short words – here.' She pulled a red pen out of the dusty vase of pens and pencils next to Uncle

Druce's place. 'If you find one, circle it. If you can't find any, that's fine. You'll save ink.'

Erin clutched the pen in her left hand and stared hopelessly at the front page. Short words. Three letters. Where was she going to find them in all that print? Well, not *all* that print. Just the big print. Like at the top of the page . . . Hey, there was one, right in the title! She circled it, then looked up at Aunt Joan, who had begun to clear the plates. 'Do I have to read it? Or write it down?'

'No,' said Aunt Joan. 'This is an exercise in form, not content.'

'Excuse me?'

'If I asked you to count jars, would you think I wanted you to tell me what was in them?'

She was obviously supposed to say no, so she did.

'Well, the jars are form, and the stuff in them is content. All I want is jars.' She stumped off to the kitchen.

Jars. Erin looked back at the page. Suppose it were a supermarket. If what you had to look for was little jars, without paying attention to what was in them, all you'd have to do was . . . Hey, there was one . . . wasn't it? She counted the letters, then looked at it. Yeah, she could see all three letters at once without moving her eyes. How about that. And there was a two-letter word: *by* – no, she didn't have to read it. In fact, reading the word just held you up when all you were looking for was jars of letters. There was one. Another . . . She circled away, and she must have been doing pretty well, because when Aunt Joan looked over her shoulder, she nodded instead of looking patient.

'Think how stuck we'd be without first-grade words,' she said. 'Can you count those circles, or do numbers give you trouble?'

'Numbers are OK – at least, as long as I don't have to write them down.'

'Nobody's going to make you write them down. Count away.'

She counted, circling a few she'd missed before as she went over the page. 'Thirty-eight.'

'Hmm,' said Aunt Joan, frowning. 'I got thirty-six – no, I see! Those two in the index. What sharp eyes you have! OK, that's it for structure today; you're on your own. I've got to go shopping before Druce gets home for lunch; the piano tuner's coming at two. Ever see a piano being tuned?'

Erin shook her head.

'Well, stick around when he comes,' said Aunt Joan, 'and you'll learn something new. Never does anybody any harm.'

The piano tuner's name was Mr Cornfield, but he didn't look like a farmer; he was tall and thin and grey – even his face, somehow – and from the moment he walked into the living room, you could tell that he felt about pianos the way Uncle Druce felt about bottle caps. He looked the piano all over outside, nodding to himself; then he propped up the lid and clicked his tongue.

'A Depression Steinway B,' he said admiringly to Aunt Joan. 'You don't see many of them these days.'

'It may need work,' she said, almost apologetically. 'It just sat there in the old family house while my step-mother – that's Druce's mother – lingered on. Sad for everybody.'

Mr Cornfield played a scale, then a few chords. Peering over the back of the shabby chair closest to the piano, Erin saw for the first time what made a piano like this play: little felt hammers came up from under-neath the strings and hit them; as they dropped back, the black things on top of the strings moved down to stop the sound – except when he used the pedal, and all the black things stayed up.

'Not bad,' he said. 'All it needs is exercise. Play it for a couple of months and you won't know it for the same instrument.'

Erin stared at him. Did pianos actually *need* to be played? He didn't seem to be joking, and Aunt Joan nodded as if she agreed.

Mr Cornfield reached into his box of tools, took out something that looked like a fork with long prongs, and held it out to her in a way that told her he knew she'd been watching. 'Know what this is?'

Erin shook her head.

'It's a tuning fork. Listen.' He knocked the prongs against his wrist and set the base on the piano. An A pulsed into the room, its vibrations humming and throbbing.

Mr Cornfield's grey mouth smiled. 'Like that, huh? Want to try it?'

Erin looked at Aunt Joan, who nodded with the kind of impatient look that warned you she might say something about creeping around like a ghost. So she walked towards the piano.

Mr Cornfield took another, larger tuning fork out of his box and handed it to her.

'Try this one; it's easier. Hold it just below where the two tines come together here, see? That way, your hand doesn't get in the way when you put it on the piano.'

Erin held it carefully and tapped it on her right wrist. The tines quivered in her hand – then, as she touched the bottom to the piano, throbbed into the room as a middle C. It was magical – as mysterious, as unexplainable as the castle in the window. Out of ordinary, everyday stuff, something wonderful suddenly appeared . . . and died away, just as completely. Except if you had one of these wonderful forks, you could make it happen again and again. Looking quickly at Mr Cornfield to be sure it was all right, she tried it again, a little harder; this time, the sound conjured up echoes from the inside of the piano.

Mr Cornfield glanced at Aunt Joan. 'Looks like you have a musician, here.'

'It runs in the Family,' said Aunt Joan. 'Along with other, less salutary things.'

'These days, they say it's all in the genes,' he said. 'But I'm still old-fashioned enough to say it's like grace – a free gift.' He held out his hand for the tuning fork, and when Erin handed it to him, his smile wasn't grey at all. 'Eight, ten years from now, if you want to be a piano tuner, let me know, OK? I'll be needing a partner about then.'

Erin wasn't sure exactly how serious he was, so she just smiled and went back to her chair as he turned to the piano. Aunt Joan threw her a 'don't-bug-him' look and stumped towards the dining room, leaving him to work, and her to watch.

Or listen, rather. All there was to watch was a grey man standing in front of the piano, fiddling with what looked like a cross between a hammer and a wrench, a couple of thin rubber strips, and some long, thin wedges. But the sound . . . !

First there was the pure sound of the tuning fork's C; then the out-of-tune wobble of vibrations as he played what was supposed to be the C on the piano. The wobble happened because the little hammers underneath hit *three* strings, not just one, and each one was out of tune in a little different way. Mr Cornfield stuck one of the rubber wedges between two of those strings, which shut them up; then he fitted the hammer-wrench over one of the black pins in front of the piano and turned it as he thumped the key. The pitch went a little too high . . . a little too low . . . there. But now, when he moved the rubber wedge from between the other two strings, the sound *really* jangled . . . ouch. He replaced the wedge, moved the hammer-wrench to another black pin, and fiddled with it until the two strings matched. When he finished with the third, it was a perfect middle C, like the tuning fork – only with a completely different texture, of course.

She rested her chin on the chair back, waiting for him to tune the piano's other Cs, but instead, he played the C together with a G, then with an F – intervals, they were called, and she *should* know what they were. Thirds? Fourths? Fifths? People talked about them all time, but you were supposed to learn which was which by writing them on a staff,* and that meant faking, not learning. This was entirely different. You could *hear* the way the vibrations were off at first, then, as he tuned one string at a time, you could gradually hear – or was it feel? – them suddenly hum together. How could you write that down? There was nothing to see; it was all what you heard; a giant design of pitches attaching each note on the piano to all the others, so when you played them together, they'd sound just right . . . She curled up in the chair, closing her eyes as she listened to the network of sounds spread from Cs to Fs, to As, to Es. A castle built with sounds instead of stones. Invisible, but there, really there. A castle in a window . . .

When she opened her eyes, the sound was entirely different. Instead of bare intervals and pitches, there

*A 'stave' is known as a 'staff' in America.

was music; and the piano was in tune. For Pete's sakes! She'd gone to sleep! Mr Cornfield would think she'd been bored . . . at least, he would if he'd noticed her. He might not have. When he was tuning, you could *see* him programme out everything but the way the sounds worked together. So maybe, if she turned round quietly and looked over the chair, he'd think she'd been listening all the time.

But it wasn't Mr Cornfield playing the piano. It was Aunt Joan, which meant he'd finished and left, maybe laughing at her . . . but that wasn't the worst thing. Looking at his tool box, she'd realized he might be the person to ask what a soldering iron was; but of course she'd been going to wait until after he was done. And now . . . !

Aunt Joan came to the end of the piece she'd been playing and looked up. 'Hello,' she said, smiling. 'Have a good nap?'

Erin looked down at the shabby patterned rug. 'I didn't mean to—'

'Don't look so hang-dog, for heaven's sake! Some societies consider the siesta a sign of civilization!' Shaking her head, Aunt Joan picked up a yellow-covered music book from out of a carton next to the bench. 'I got down my old music from the attic,' she said. 'A lot of it is too difficult for you — not to mention for me, these days — but there's enough to keep you in tunes for the summer.' She set the book on the music rack and began to play. 'You know this?'

It took Erin a few bars to realize it was a piece Rob had worked on, because Aunt Joan played it . . . well, differently. But slowly, she nodded. 'I've heard it,' she said, suddenly thinking of Con. 'But I don't know who wrote it or anything.'

'Bach wrote it,' said Aunt Joan, still playing. 'It's the first prelude in *The Well-tempered Clavier* – the hymn he wrote to celebrate figuring out how to tune a piano.'

Erin would have laughed if Aunt Joan had said that this morning; but now, after hearing all those wonderful intervals, she understood why Bach would want to write a hymn about it. And in a way, the hymn was like the piano-tuning – a pattern, growing and growing. Erin pillowed her cheek on her hands, transfixed, as the sound castle got more complicated and exciting, then faded away slowly through an amazing arch that led to a gently closed gate.

Aunt Joan looked up from the keyboard. 'You could play this, if you thought about it right. It's just chords, and they lie under your hand very easily. The trick is not to play it clunkily – but you could figure that out after you'd learned the notes. Come over here, so I can show you how it works.'

How it works. Another lesson – on note-reading, this time. But nobody would dream of disobeying Aunt Joan, so Erin scrambled out of the chair, trying to ignore the way her stomach felt, and stared attentively at the music on the piano's rack.

Aunt Joan glanced up. 'I thought you said you couldn't read notes.'

'I did.'

'Well, then, don't *look* at them, for heaven's sake! Look at the keyboard – what's wrong?'

'Um, nothing. It's just . . . I didn't think that was allowed. My teacher said—'

'*Don't look at the keys, Erin! Look at the music!*' barked Aunt Joan, so sharply that Erin jumped. Then, more softly, 'Is that right?'

'Yeah.'

'Well, that's what you tell kids when you give lessons,' said Aunt Joan. 'I've said it myself, often enough. But not to everybody. People learn things in different ways; that means they notice different things. Like you, for instance.' She smiled a strange kind of smile, almost as if she were a kid. 'You know perfectly well the pattern on the keyboard helps you remember what you hear – for heaven's sake, Erin! Don't look so *guilty*!'

'I . . . I'm sorry.'

Aunt Joan sighed. 'Try not to say that, all right? Apologies really get under my skin. It has to do with the Family and its heritage, but I'll spare you the details. All you need to know is that in *this* house, as I said this morning, *what* you see always counts, to which I now add: *how* you see things is just fine. OK?'

Erin nodded quickly. Anything to keep Aunt Joan from exploding!

'Now, look at the keys while I play. It's chords – see? Here's the first one, which you play twice. Then there's this one – twice again – then this one twice, then back to home. Watch again, then listen as I break them up.'

Aunt Joan's hands were covered with strange brown freckles and blue veins, and her knuckles were huge and swollen, but her fingers knew where they were going. 'See how it works?' she said, looking up.

'I . . . I think so.'

'Good. Now I'll get up, and you try it. Just those four sets of chords; no more.'

Erin sat down, put her fingers over the notes Aunt Joan had played last, and pushed the keys down. It was the right chord, but it sounded as if her hands were shaking – which they were – and this wonderful piano deserved lots more than wimpy playing. Once more. There, that was better.

'Good,' said Aunt Joan. 'Now, hear the next chord in your head, think of where my hands went, and play it.'

Hear it in your head. Think of where my hands went. Erin's fingers shook so hard she could hardly move them to the right place, and though she knew the notes would be right if she pushed the keys down, she couldn't make herself do it.

'That's perfect,' said Aunt Joan encouragingly. 'Go ahead!'

Go ahead. Go ahead and do what everybody else told her was wrong, bad, deceitful – play what you heard and memorize the way it looked. Mrs Fenway, her piano teacher; Dr Goldberg, the psychologist; Mom, Dad – what would they all say if they knew the minute they weren't around, she started doing what they said she mustn't do, ever ever?

'Erin, honey – what's the matter?'

Aunt Joan didn't sound angry. Maybe, if she just explained, without apologizing or anything . . . She drew a long, shaky breath. 'It's faking.'

'Faking! How can it be?'

'I'm not reading the notes.'

'But you're not *pretending* to read the notes! That's what's faking! Here—' Aunt Joan lifted the music book off the rack. 'There! Now you *can't* read the notes, so you can't possibly be trying to fool anybody.'

Erin stared at the empty music rack. That made sense – or at least it seemed to. But you had to be very careful when people seemed to make sense about doing things that were wrong. Everybody knew that.

'Erin. Do you understand what I'm saying?'

She nodded; of course she understood. And there were her fingers, all ready to play that wonderful chord, which didn't feel wrong at all. But if Aunt Joan was right, what about what everybody *else* had said? How could you tell for certain whether somebody was leading you down the right path or the wrong one? Other people seemed to know, but probably *they* could see the difference between right and wrong, whereas for her, it was as unseeable as the difference between right and left. She looked desperately up at Aunt Joan's blurred, wavering face. 'I . . . I can't . . .'

'OK,' said Aunt Joan, her voice tight and dry. 'Go on upstairs and play with the knights or something. You can take this with you, if you want. It was in the box with the music.' She reached in the pocket of her shabby skirt and drew out a tuning fork.

'Thank you,' Erin croaked over the dry place in her throat. 'I'll be very careful with it.' And to prove that she would, she didn't let herself run up to her room and disappear. She walked, keeping her shoulders straight and her head back, and at the top of the stairs she went where Aunt Joan had said to go.

7
'Three Blind Mice'

When she got to the little room, she shut the door behind her and leaned against it, slowly raising her eyes from the toy boxes to the window. It looked just the way it had this morning when she'd checked it out; big, with panes of slightly wavering old-fashioned glass that looked out over the overgrown garden, the falling-down fence, and the peeling clapboard of the house next door. Well, that was nothing to cry about; she hadn't *really* expected anything different. Besides, Uncle Druce's study door was open, and crying would disturb him. Not to mention, Aunt Joan had been upset – anybody could tell that – and sometimes when people were upset about something you'd done, they came up to talk to you after they'd had a few minutes to think things over rationally. So no crying. And she'd better get a few knights out, so there wouldn't be any questions.

Quickly, she unwrapped Sir Piers, Malachi and the

knight and put them on their toy box next to the tuning fork. That would do it— No, wait! What if Aunt Joan started out by being sort of casual and friendly, the way people did sometimes, and asked to see the rest of the knights? That just *couldn't* happen yet; there had to be time to find out about soldering irons and how you used them instead of glue. She could even buy one, maybe; Mom had given her a lot of money.

Yeah, but what could she do right now? She looked at Sir Piers, hoping he'd inspire her – and maybe he did, because she suddenly saw. Sure! How simple! Build a castle *on top* of the toy box, and say it was like the picture in the Tennyson book. Nobody would make her move it if she did that! Smiling gratefully at Sir Piers, she reached for the book behind him and opened it to the picture, then laid the tuning fork on it to keep it from shutting. For a few minutes, she studied the castle, then she opened the second toy box and began to take out pieces. Big, thick walls around the outside, two blocks thick, but not lined up exactly; that would be like tuning a piano with only Cs. She began to place them around the outside of the lid; but after she got one ring of plain blocks, she found a bunch of pillars and arches further down in the box . . . hey, maybe she could put *those* on the inside wall, building a row of stables, like Sir Piers's real castle. She set them up, and they looked unbelievably cool – but anybody could see they were going to fall down if they had only one row of blocks around the outside.

She looked at them. What could she do? Rob would know. Dad would know. Even Mom would have an idea. But she . . . ! She picked up the tuning fork and tapped it against her wrist in absent-minded frustration as the page fluttered shut.

Hummmmm.

Her eyes slid from the closed book to the tines. With a hum like that, you'd expect them to quiver more than they did. She moved it closer to her face and heard the hum melt into a private A, just for her. But of course it was louder if you set its base on something, like a block. She tapped it on her wrist and tried again, but the A didn't sound nearly as wonderful as it had sounded on the piano. Maybe it needed something hollow. Like a toy box. She set the tuning fork's base next to Sir Piers, and saw him quiver as the A shimmered into the room. Again. Again. If you gave the tuning fork a real whack before you set it down, *everything* hummed, even the window.

She looked up to watch the pane vibrate – blinked – and looked again.

Slowly, the peeling clapboard of the house next door got dimmer; superimposed on it, very lightly, the way reflections looked in daytime windows, there was . . . She strained her eyes, waiting for stones, battlements, flags, but all that seemed to be there was something black, and the half-developed sound of music, so faint and far away that she looked down at the tuning fork clutched in her fingers, then hesitantly tapped it on her wrist and set it next to Sir Piers again to see if that was it. Hummmm . . .

The windowpane shivered, grew clearer. Erin scrambled to her feet and walked slowly towards it. On the other side, there was an enormous room filled with rays of sunlight slanting in through tall windows . . . but not castle windows. And at the far end of the room, half silhouetted against the light where three windows formed a bay, there was a grand piano ... no, two grand pianos, side by side. And sitting at the nearest one – the one with its lid up – was a pianist, playing music that started out sounding like Mozart and gradually turned to jazz, then stopped altogether as he looked her way. A pianist with a thin face, big hands and feet, and cowlicky hair. Con. She jumped onto the sill, looked back once to be sure the room was still there, then stepped down.

He pushed the bench back and stared at her, his face gradually lighting up. 'Error! How did you get here?'

'Same way I'm going to leave,' she said, 'if that's what you're going to call me.'

'Aw, c'mon,' he said. 'It's just a pun.'

'Sure. And your name is Con-descension. Ha, ha.'

Con winced. 'OK, OK. Erin, as in Ireland, not Error as in wrong. Not close at all, unless you're a master pundit. Which reminds me of my speciality in word games. How about a fine round of Hink Pink? It might cheer you up.'

'What makes you think I need cheering up?'

'I forgot to tell you, ESP is one of my talents. Unlike some of the others, it never fails. Now to play Hink Pink, one person thinks of something and the other has to describe it in two words that rhyme with each other.'

Oh brother. Just what she needed. 'Um . . . is this like a spelling bee?'

'A spelling bee! You *still* think I'm an ogre? This is different. Listen, what do you call Shakespeare after a knife fight?'

She shook her head.

'A *scarred bard*. And a wicked clergyman is a *sinister minister*.' He looked at her closely. 'No? Not cheered up? Well, remember what I was telling you about improvising, but I couldn't show you because there wasn't a piano? Here's a piano. If you want, I could show you now.'

You might learn something new. Never did anybody any harm. 'Well . . .'

'Great!' Con plopped down on the bench and pulled it forward. 'Let's start with a simple tune – "Three Blind Mice", for example. First, you just play it, in C, probably, since it's easiest for beginners, but improvising works in any key you want. Here we go.' He played the first two bars, then looked up. 'Got it?'

'Yeah,' she said, frowning a bit. 'But if you want to teach me how to do it in C, you'd better *play* it in C, or I'll get mixed up.'

'OK,' he said, and played the next two bars in E flat, watching her out of the corner of his eye.

'Come *on*!' she said. 'You were going to show me *something*, not show *off*.'

'I wasn't showing off!' he said indignantly. 'I *said* you didn't have to play it in C, so I was demonstrating . . . and then when you noticed, I said to myself, hey, is she watching my hands, or does she have perfect pitch? Do you?'

'What's perfect pitch?'

'Knowing what key something's in, just from listening to it . . . No, that's not right. It's . . . Look. Close your eyes – tight, so I know you can't see my hands, OK? Then I'll play a note, and you tell me what it is.'

What on earth . . . ? But she closed her eyes, and he played a note. 'G,' she said. 'The one below middle C.'

'Yeah?' he said, his voice sounding sort of excited. 'What about these two?' He thumped a note way up in the treble, then way down in the bass.

'C sharp,' she said. 'Then E flat – can I open my eyes, now?'

'Sure,' he said, and when she opened them, she saw he was looking at her with something like respect. 'I'll be darned,' he said. 'You can do that, and nobody's *noticed*?'

'Why on earth would they? If I can do it, *anybody* can.'

'Like heck they can! Listen, Error . . . Erin . . . when it comes to perfect pitch, you're talking about maybe one person in ten thousand!'

She thought of the way Rob sang and the way Dad whistled off-key. She'd always wondered how they could do it, but . . . She looked at Con. 'But *you* can do it, can't you? I mean, you knew how to test me.'

'Sure, I can do it. But you can bet people noticed. My dad – like I said, he was a pianist; all of us kids could sing any note he played before we were two – but he was especially excited about me, because as soon as I learned the keyboard, all he had to do was point to a key, and I could sing its note before he played it.'

She looked at him wonderingly. 'And that's perfect pitch?'

'Yep. And if you've got it, you're a natural for improvising, because it starts with harmonizing. Watch, now. I start by playing chords in the bass that go with the tune in the treble.' He played, and sure enough, the stupid little mice had an accompaniment.

'That's all there is to it?'

'Not on your life! That's just harmony – absolutely dull, but absolutely important. Listen – I'll play it in C minor, now . . .' He grinned and made the little mice sound sad. 'Or I'll play it in three-quarter time . . .' The mice suddenly danced a waltz. 'See? Once you've got the basic harmony down, you can turn the tune into anything you want. That's what's so much fun about it. Listen.'

He took off, his hands flying up and down the keyboard. And although she knew he was showing off, she listened, spellbound. 'Three Blind Mice' as jazz.

'Three Blind Mice' as Mozart. 'Three Blind Mice' as a hymn. She'd had no idea *anybody* could do that on a piano – let alone a kid. How exciting it would be to do it yourself! Except . . .

Con thundered down the piano in octave runs that made the mice into a flashy concerto with twelve huge chords at the end. 'There!' he said. 'So now— Hey, what's the matter?'

'You're not reading music. People've told me that was wrong.'

'*What!!*'

'I said—'

'I heard you,' he said. 'I was just surprised. I mean, you're not dumb, and you have this *terrific* ear – so how can you possibly believe that the only way to play music is to read what's on a page?'

It did sound kind of funny, if you put it that way. 'Well, I—'

But he rolled right over her. 'Take just one cotton-pickin' moment to think, all right? If the only music is on the page, *where did the music Bach wrote come from before he wrote it down*?'

She stared at him, her mind swirling . . . then suddenly, it wasn't just her mind. Everything else started swirling too; then suddenly a door opened behind her. Whirling round, she saw Aunt Joan standing in the hall.

'Something interesting going on out there?' she said, glancing at the window.

Erin glanced over her shoulder; the window was just a window. Dizzily, she steadied herself on the frame. 'No,' she said, trying to smile. 'I was just looking out at the garden.'

That was a pretty poor cover-up, and Aunt Joan *must* know that, but all she did was look a little sad. 'We've really got to get you outside more,' she said, sighing. 'All work and no play . . . that sort of thing. But what I came up here to tell you and Druce – since calling didn't do any good – was that dinner's ready. Let's go eat it while it's still tepid.'

8
Hink Pink

At home, if you didn't finish everything on your plate, people asked you what was wrong – and how could you possibly explain you weren't hungry because your head was still spinning from coming back through a window that wasn't a window? But here, it turned out not to be a problem. Uncle Druce was absorbed in his catalogues, and after a few minutes of silence, Aunt Joan sighed and picked up a magazine, which left plenty of time to think. If thinking was the word for it. It was more like one of those tunes you couldn't get rid of than a thought: Con's voice, over and over – '*If the only music is on the page, where did the music Bach wrote come from before he wrote it down?*'

Obviously, the answer was 'Out of Bach's head.' Or maybe, 'Out of Bach's fingers.' She looked at her potatoes, but what she saw was the way Con's fingers flashed over the keyboard. That wasn't thought, either; his hands just *knew* where to go. He'd practised lots, of course, but not the kind of practice Rob did, carefully learning the music from the page, as if it were directions, and following them. Con's fingers were attached to his mind. They *made things up*, like Bach. For sure, that had to be different from faking.

A magazine rustled; glancing to the side, Erin met Aunt Joan's eyes and quickly took a bite to get rid of the worried look in them. But that didn't work in the long run; during dishes, Aunt Joan told Uncle Druce that it was unnatural for a child to sit around the house all day, and after considering a while, he said, well, there was that bike in the garage. So as soon as they found the garage key, all three of them went out to look at it. Or look *for* it, anyway. The garage was so full of boxes and old furniture and tools and newspapers waiting to get recycled that there wasn't any room for the car any more, and the bike was way at the back. But eventually, Uncle Druce wheeled it out into the violets and propped it up with a stand that came down from the frame.

'Looks OK to me,' he said. 'Just needs a clean-up – here.' He handed Aunt Joan the red bandanna handkerchief that usually poked out of his back pocket. 'Lemme see if I can find a pump for those tyres.' He shambled back into the garage.

Aunt Joan unfolded the bandanna. 'It's going to take more cleaning than this can do,' she said, smiling. 'But it's a good bike – took me back and forth to school for years. They don't make them like this any more.'

They sure didn't. It was heavy and black, with a chain guard, fenders and (would you believe) *baskets* on each side of the back wheel. An antique. Amazing.

Uncle Druce appeared again with a big, clumsy bicycle pump and went to work on the tyres. When he'd finished, he pulled a wrench from his pocket, made her stand next to the bike, and lowered the seat and handlebars.

'There!' he said. 'Wheel it out in front and jump on, so we can see if those tyres'll hold up until I get them new tubes.'

Looking at him, she realized that saying she didn't have a clue how to ride a bike like this wouldn't just be rude – it would hurt his feelings. It had been his idea, and he was standing there, interested in something that wasn't bottle caps for the first time since she'd met him. So she smiled, wheeled it out the gate and rode it down the sidewalk. It felt more like a tank than a bike, and she couldn't figure out how to change gears, so her feet whirled around too fast, but she didn't fall over, and when she got back to the house, Uncle Druce looked so pleased it was almost worth it.

'Here,' he said, taking it from her. 'I'll put it in the garage – got to hunt up its old chain and lock, so you can leave it by the pond, or wherever.'

She thanked him politely, but what he'd said didn't sink in until she went inside and Aunt Joan said, 'There! Now you can go exploring! Granted, it's not an exciting town, but there's a park not too far down the street; that's where the pond is. And the other way is downtown – not much traffic if you go in the middle of the day.'

Explore. A park. A pond. Downtown. 'You mean, *by myself*?'

'Of course, by yourself,' said Aunt Joan. 'That's much the most—' She switched on the light and frowned. 'Exploring isn't a new thing for you, is it?'

'Um . . . well, the city isn't safe. And the psychologist told Mom about spatial disorientation, where kids like me have trouble with maps and get lost easily, so—'

'—So she never allowed you out unchaperoned?' said Aunt Joan, with a touch of acid in her voice. 'Not even to go round the corner and buy a bottle of milk or a newspaper?'

'Well, with Rob—'

'But never alone?'

Erin shook her head, feeling her stomach turn over as she waited for an Aunt Joanism. But Aunt Joan's voice, when it came, was almost gentle.

'Well, if that's the case,' she said, 'start with little trips. If you *really* get disoriented, tell me and we'll work on the map-maker in your head. But a lot of it is just finding out you can do it. Up to bed, now; it's long after eight.'

Up to bed it was, and though Erin woke up twice and tiptoed into the little room, there was nothing – absolutely nothing – going on with the window. And as if that weren't bad enough, listening for music kept you from really sleeping, so you dreamed. Not about castles, either. About streets — miles and miles of them, opening into each other like mazes, all marked with signs you couldn't read because you were too stupid.

'OK,' said Aunt Joan after Uncle Druce had left for work. 'Today we work on content, not form.' Her stiff fingers opened an old carton and awkwardly drew out — shoot! It was a set of magnetic letters like Mom used to put on the refrigerator, and one of those green magnetic boards you could stick them on. Like for three-year-olds.

Aunt Joan dumped the letters on the table. 'You know what? This is how people were taught to read in Shakespeare's time. Not with plastic, of course; that's a modern atrocity. But they used wooden blocks with letters on them.'

'Really?'

'Absolutely. Don't know who thought of it, but my hat is off to them, because they understood that to read, you have to see patterns in words, and that to *see* patterns, it helps to *make* them.' She smiled an Aunt Joan kind of smile. 'So you're going to do what Shakespeare had to do at some point, which is take an *a* and a *d* out of the pile and stick them on the board so they say *ad.*'

Erin fished out the letters, wondering what Shakespeare had been like when he was a kid. It seemed almost wrong to think of him *learning* things, though of course he'd had to . . . She put the *a* and the *d* on the board and looked up.

'You sure those say *ad*, not *da*?' said Aunt Joan.

Oh, no! She'd done it backwards! Erin's hands jumped to switch the letters.

'Wait!' said Aunt Joan. 'I didn't say it was wrong. I asked you if *you* were sure it was right. Are you?'

How did you explain you were *never* sure?

'OK,' said Aunt Joan. 'Let me show you a way of being sure.' She pulled a little notebook out of the box the letters had been in and wrote:

ad da

'Now watch,' she said. 'Suppose I draw lines around them, like this—'

'—*ad* looks like a sofa, with a seat and a back, right? But *da*—'

'Oh, I see!' said Erin. 'There's a seat on each side!'

'You've got it,' said Aunt Joan, looking pleased. 'And I promise you, every *ad* you see – given the absence of some peculiar type font – will look like a sofa if you draw a line around it. So look back at the board; is it right?'

'Yes.'

'Good. Now, let's take *ad* and make it into something else by adding letters to the side with the sofa seat.' She fished a letter out of the pile and put it in front of the *ad*. 'What's that say?'

'*Lad?*'

'You sure?'

Erin checked again. She was pretty sure. 'Yeah.'

'Good. Why does it say *lad* instead of *bad* or *mad*?'

This was very confusing. 'Because of the *l*.'

'You're getting there. What sound does *l* make? Say *ad*, then *lad*.'

'*Lad. Ad* – oh. The *luh* sound?'

'Right. Every letter has a sound – when you put them together, their sounds mix, like chords on a piano, but instead of chords, you get words.' Aunt Joan picked up a *p* from the pile and put it where the *l* had been. '*P* says *puh*. So what word is it now?'

'*Puh-ad* – oh! *Pad*!' It couldn't be this easy. 'Does it always work?'

'Not always.' Aunt Joan took an *x* out of the pile and made the *pad* into *xad*. 'No chord, just three notes jangling together, right? But a lot of letters will make a word if you put them in front of *ad*. While I clear these dishes, you fiddle around with the alphabet and try each letter. Keep the letters that make word-chords. Got that?'

Erin nodded. She did get it. And unlike most stuff people made you do about reading, it was interesting. Words as chords of letters. Words as sounds. They were sure easier to deal with if you thought of them like that. *Aad*. That was silly. But *b-ad*, *c-ad* (what did that mean, anyway?), *d-ad*, *l-ad*, *m-ad* . . . *mad dad*. An angry father. Hey, yeah! And if you lost a Paddington Bear at the railway station, you had a *sad Pad*.

'Looks like you're getting the idea,' said Aunt Joan, coming back for the last of the dishes. 'Haven't seen you smile like that since you came.'

Things went so well in the morning that she began to hope that everyone had forgotten about the bike, but her luck ran out after lunch. Right after Uncle Druce had shambled upstairs, Aunt Joan said, 'Time for fresh air and exercise. I have to go shopping pretty soon, but since this is your maiden voyage as an explorer, I figured I'd wait until you got back before I left.'

'Um . . . uh, fine.'

'Sure, you'll be fine. You're an intelligent child – and I assume you've already figured out that the easiest way of not getting lost is to go straight. Then there won't be any turns to worry about coming back.'

How did you explain that the other night you'd walked straight along a parapet and down some stairs

95

– and gotten totally lost coming home?

Aunt Joan picked up her newspaper. 'You'll also get to the park, if you keep going for ten or twelve blocks. The street runs right into it; and you can see the pond and the trees from where you'll be. Run along, now.'

Run along. Heck, her heart was thumping so hard she could hardly stand up. But for sure, Aunt Joan would tell Aunt Agatha and the others terrible things about Mom if she looked frightened, so Erin made herself smile as she pedalled slowly towards the first cross street away from town. That's when she found out that getting lost was only one of the problems explorers faced; another one was getting run over. There were no traffic lights in this stupid town! If a car came along a cross street, what happened? She stopped as she came to the first one, looking around. There was no stop sign on her street; but there was on the cross street – she couldn't read it from where she was, but it was the right shape. OK, so Aunt Joan's street was the important one, and all the others had stop signs. She rode on, feeling much safer, until she came the next street. And there was a stop sign, big as life.

She stopped, which was a good thing, because a car whizzed by without even slowing down. Jeez. Carefully, she edged the bike forward, looking both ways, then crossed the street and went on. Her feet were still going round too fast, and there weren't any gear-levers on the frame. But what about the little gizmo on the handlebars? That had a lever. She coasted for a second, fiddling with it – watch out! Watch out! Another cross street! She squeezed the brakes so hard she nearly went over the handlebars, but there were no cars. No stop sign, either. If only Rob were there! He'd know which ones you were supposed to stop at and which ones you weren't! She shoved off . . . and hey, the pedals were harder to push, and she was riding at a decent speed, now – yikes! *Another* cross street . . . but with no stop sign on her street. Just on the other.

All of a sudden, it dawned on her, and it was so simple she turned bright red, even though nobody was around. Of course. People didn't want to run into each other here, any more than they did in the city, so they put signs on one street or the other. When there wasn't a sign on your street, you didn't have to stop, and you *knew* there was one on the other street. All you had to do was look for signs, and that was all Rob would have done if he'd been with her. There wasn't any kind of magic to understanding those things, then. A lot of it was just paying attention. Even she could do that.

There were bike rides every day after that, and she always got back OK. Once you'd learned to look back on the way out so you knew what it would look like going the other way, being on your own got less scary and even sort of nice. You could look at flower gardens without anybody telling you to hurry up, watch kids playing without being told to join them, and sit with your feet dangling in the pond without anybody

97

worrying about rusty tin cans . . . and you could play Hink Pink with all those rhyming words in your reading lesson. Or think about how to get back to Sir Piers or Con.

She thought about that a lot, because no matter how often she checked, the window stayed a window, and she was afraid of checking too often, because eventually Aunt Joan and Uncle Druce were bound to ask what was up, and then they'd find out the knights were broken. After a week, she decided she'd be extra brave and ride downtown and look for the kind of shop where you might buy soldering irons. But the next day – wouldn't you know – it rained cats and dogs.

The morning wasn't a total loss, though, because Aunt Joan had some kind of meeting at ten, so she took off right after reading lesson. The minute Erin was alone, she raced up to the little room and tried all the plans she thought of by the pond. Setting up the toy Sir Piers and Malachi on a special pile of blocks. Opening the Tennyson book to all the castle-iest pictures. Laying out a thin, flat block (a drawbridge, probably) on top of two regular ones to make a sounding board, and making the whole room hum with the tuning fork. But though she waited very patiently, nothing happened.

There had to be some connection she wasn't making. She looked wistfully at Sir Piers . . . And suddenly, as if he'd told her, she knew what it was. The piano! Every time the window had changed, she'd played the piano earlier in the day. Which she'd stopped doing, because . . . well, mostly because Aunt Joan had played Bach's hymn to piano-tuning quite a bit. That was a hint, and you had to be very firm about not noticing hints; sometimes they were sneaky ways of making kids do what grown-ups wanted.

Yeah, but nobody was hinting now, and nobody was listening but Sir Piers and Malachi. She hurried down the stairs between the bottle-cap boxes – and the minute she sat down at the piano, she knew for certain this was it. The wonderful sound filled the house, right up to the little room; you could *feel* everything coming to life. She played every piece she knew, and she was about to start all over again when she suddenly realized that the last time the window had opened up, she'd been playing – or at least starting – Bach's hymn to piano-tuning. Maybe she should forget hints, faking and all that confusing stuff, and give it a whirl, as Con would say, just in case. She placed her fingers over the keys Aunt Joan had showed her and pushed them down. Right. And now the next one. Right. Next. Next. Then the first one again. There.

It was so beautiful, you almost felt you weren't worthy of playing it. Think of being Bach, hearing those chords in your head – and knowing you were the *first person* to hear them. She played them five times in a row, to teach her hands the pattern. What came next? This? No. This? Yes! She went on, playing each chord, going back to be sure she had it, going on. This was lots harder than learning the pieces for her lesson; the farther into it she got, the more she forgot what came next. If only she could read music, like a normal person! Think of what she could play then! She plopped her hands down on the keyboard in a despairing blob of sound and stared off into the dining room.

And saw Uncle Druce sitting in his place, sorting.

She'd been playing that long? She hadn't heard him come in? She looked at him dizzily, feeling the way she had when she'd whisked back through the window.

Aunt Joan stumped into the dining room with a tray. 'Glad to see you found yourself something to do,' she said, as if nothing special had happened. 'You're stuck where everybody gets stuck — those difficult transitional chords — but it's only two more bars to the wonderful progression that leads to the end. I'll show you later, if you want.'

Erin got up and walked slowly across towards the dining room, not sure what to say. Luckily, Aunt Joan just passed her a sandwich, and Uncle Druce kept on sorting without even looking up, so she didn't have to say anything at all.

9
Swordplay

It rained all afternoon, and at night it turned into a huge thunderstorm – lightning like Rob's seventies strobe lamp, long drum-rolls of thunder, and wind that made the old shabby house shudder. Erin lay in bed, watching it over the bump of her feet, ready to shut her eyes if Aunt Joan came in to see if she was scared, but there wasn't a sound in the house. Except . . . was that singing?

She jumped out of bed, listening. *Flash. BOOMmmrumblerumblerumble.* But there *was* somebody singing, and with all the noise outside, it couldn't possibly be a radio. She'd been right, then – the piano *was* the key to the castle! She padded quickly down the flickering hall to the little room and closed its door behind her. Instantly, the storm noises stopped, and the lightning flashes in the window disappeared in a swirling dark grey fog. Gradually, the swirls grew lighter and thinner . . . then suddenly, wonderfully, the castle parapet loomed before her, its battlements huge and dark against a late-afternoon sun. Erin rushed forward and jumped on the sill, listening. It was Sir Piers's voice, all right – one of them was, anyway; there was another voice, too. They were coming from below, probably from that room where she'd found him before.

Glancing up at the towers, she saw a pair of guards. They didn't see her, but just in case, she slipped along the shadowed side of the parapet to the tower door. As she started down the twisting staircase, the sound of a lute drifted up to meet her, and soon Sir Piers's voice followed it with a new song.

> *'Sumer is i-cumen in,*
> *Lhude singe cuckoo.'*

She wanted to rush right down, but this was where she'd gotten mixed up last time, and her bike rides had taught her how to keep from getting lost on the way home: look back carefully. Turning round every few steps, she scrutinized the layout of the staircase as she made her way down: three passages off to the side, then finally the familiar arch, and Sir Piers's wonderful room. She tiptoed into the space behind the half-open door and peered cautiously around it.

Sir Piers was sitting where he'd sat before, with Malachi at his feet. Near him, dressed in crimson, was a boy a couple of years younger than Rob, with an interesting, sharp face and brown shoulder-length hair. It had to be Giles, the squire whose arrival William had announced. As she watched, Sir Piers started the cuckoo song over again, and after he'd sung the first line, he pointed at Giles, who came in, singing the same words. A round! Cool. She edged forward, listening eagerly as the two voices mingled. Sir Piers reached the end first, of course, and he stopped while Giles finished alone. Then he played two chords on his lute and laughed. 'Your father has taught you all his old tricks, Giles. Only Malachi follows more closely!'

'My father and I played this game all the time,' said Giles, smiling. 'Let me lead now. Here is one I fancy even you don't know.' And he began.

> 'Ding-dong, ding-dong dell.
> Pussy's in the well.
> Pussy's in the well.
> Ding-dong, ding-dong dell.'

After he'd sung it once, he started again, pointing to Sir Piers at the end of the first line. As Sir Piers came in, Erin realized how the game worked: the point was to sing the round through after you'd heard it only *once*, so you had to listen very carefully to the line ahead of you while you were singing yours, or you'd get lost. That was hard – especially with a round like this, which had a difficult skip in the middle. But Sir

Piers followed easily, and it sounded so lovely that they sang it all the way through twice.

When they finished, Sir Piers looked at the boy seriously over his lute. 'Your gift is great,' he said. 'And your training a testimony to your father's talents. Are you certain that you wish to be a knight, not a bard?'

'Must I choose?' said Giles gaily. 'My father said that your deeds proved a great bard can also be the finest of knights, and no wonder, for their skills are the same. Like a bard, a knight needs patience, practice, dedication, a well-taught hand and the ability to concentrate on one part while paying attention to the whole. The only difference is that a bard needs a trained ear, whereas a knight needs a trained eye.'

'Your father was a wise man,' said Sir Piers. 'And what you have just said about a trained ear and a trained eye reminds me of the last occasion on which I sorely missed him. A month or so ago, a stranger came to our gates. He was from a distant land where, he said, bards shared music not as we do, by ear, but by drawing it upon a page for other men to see and interpret. Have you heard of this?'

Erin stared as Giles shook his head. Sir Piers, who played and sang so beautifully, didn't know what written music was? Giles, who could lead and follow effortlessly in rounds, couldn't read notes? But they weren't stupid! Anybody could tell that! She looked around the room. Tapestries, benches, tables, musical instruments – but no books, no music anywhere to be seen. She blinked wonderingly and looked back at Giles, who had begun to laugh.

'I would say your stranger was mad,' he said. 'How could you draw a sound?'

'I didn't fully understand,' said Sir Piers. 'And I, too, thought perhaps he was a little mad. But later, I remembered that all new things seem mad to men who have not encountered them, and I wished your father were alive. He would have been most interested.'

'No doubt he would,' said Giles — not quite dismissively, but as if he were uncomfortable with the subject and wished to change it. 'To him, interest in all things was part of a knight's duty. But in the months before his death, his chief interest lay in training me in the arts that would make me worthy of succeeding him. He hoped to make me a knight this year.'

Sir Piers's eyebrows rose. 'This year! Musically, you are more than ready, but what of your other training? There is much to be learned with the sword and the lance — and you are very young.'

'Not too young to honour my father. Or to prove my mastery of the skills he has taught me.'

A hubbub of voices and a clash of metal rose to the window from the courtyard outside. Sir Piers looked over his shoulder, then smiled at the boy. 'If you wish to prove your command of a sword equal to your quickness of ear, now is your time.'

Giles jumped up. 'Swordplay!' he breathed. 'May I go arm myself?'

'I would recommend it,' said Sir Piers dryly. 'Swordplay without armour is a considerable risk.'

If Giles heard the irony in the knight's voice, he ignored it. 'Thank you!' he said, bowing. And he sprinted out of the room so quickly that Erin hardly had time to jump out of his way.

Sir Piers listened to his footsteps race down the stairs; then he got up, set his lute on the table of instruments, and sighed. 'Whatever the boy's skills,' he said, stroking Malachi's head as the dog rose and stood beside him, 'he is not yet a man. His father would have seen instantly what great harmonies could be created, and for how many voices, if there were a way of preserving them for all to share. Yet Giles—' He patted the dog once more. 'No, that is unfair; he has an ear for novelty. His little song is like nothing I have heard before.' He picked up one of the flutes and began to polish it, pensively singing Giles's round. '*Ding-dong, ding-dong dell . . .*'

Erin quivered as she listened. It *was* an unusual round – much more interesting than 'Row, row, row your boat' and the other ones they taught you at school. And she'd heard it a couple of times now. Shouldn't being invisible mean nobody could hear you? Could she maybe, very quietly, follow him? Watching Sir Piers closely, she came in so softly she could hardly hear her own voice. He remained absorbed in the flute and in his thoughts, singing only to himself, so she sang a little louder . . . then stopped as Malachi cocked his head and walked towards her. But it didn't do any good. He hadn't just heard her; he was looking right at the place she was standing.

Run! Run! screamed everything inside her. But fortunately, lots of the people in the Family had dogs, and she knew better than to listen to that panicky voice. Besides, he didn't look threatening; he looked puzzled. Slowly, so as not to scare him, she held out her hand, palm down. 'Hi, Malachi,' she whispered.

The dog came a step closer and lowered his head to sniff at her hand. After a few seconds, she raised the other hand and stroked him. 'You're beautiful,' she whispered. 'I wish I had a dog like you.'

He was too good a dog to be flattered by something like that, but he gave her a look of aloof recognition that told her she wouldn't have any trouble with him now, so long as—

'Phantoms again, Malachi?' said Sir Piers, laying down the flute with a frown.

Malachi ambled back to his side with a look of slightly embarrassed dignity, then cocked his head at the sound of marching feet in the courtyard.

'Yes,' said Sir Piers, 'we should go down and watch. And let us hope that the boy performs well. It will go hard with him if his father's love has inflated his opinion of his skills.'

He walked thoughtfully out of the room; Malachi trotted behind him without even a look at Erin as they passed. She listened to them go, wondering what to do.

It seemed a shame not to see if Giles was any good with a sword. Did she dare watch from the window? She would be in all sorts of trouble if somebody came in – well, probably not, if nobody could see her but a dog. That was sort of a funny feeling. Like, was she really here? Suppose she was just dreaming, or was a ghost or something, and the real her was back in the little room, all ready to 'be' there if Aunt Joan opened the door. There was a thought! Mulling it over, she tip-toed further into the room. Sir Piers's lute lay before her on the table of instruments, beautiful with its inlaid front and gourd-shaped back. Next to it, lying parallel to the wooden flute Sir Piers had been polishing, lay an unsheathed dagger. If she weren't really here, touching the point of that dagger wouldn't prick her finger. That sounded scientific. OK, then – ow! She jerked her hand back, shaking her finger. So much for that idea.

A trumpet sounded in the courtyard, and a voice began shouting what sounded like instructions. Erin looked quickly at the door; nobody was around, and there were no footsteps on the stairs. If she wanted to watch, this was as safe as she was going to get. She climbed on the bench that ran under the window and stood on tiptoe so she could see out. Below her, ten squires were standing before a knight in a red surcoat, looking for all the world like a soccer team before a coach. In spite of their chain mail and helmets, she could tell that Giles was one of them; his surcoat was crimson instead of blue, and he was half a head shorter than most of them. The knight in charge seemed to be pairing them off, and after he had called two names, Sir Piers stepped forward and spoke to him. Erin strained her eyes and ears, but she was too far away to get even a clue about what he wanted, until the squires separated into their pairs. Then she saw that Giles was paired with the only squire who was about his height. Well, that was fair, but you had to wonder how Giles felt about it.

She found out fast enough; the other squires began walking towards the open area beyond the blacksmith's shop, but the coach knight positioned Giles and his opponent in front of Sir Piers and signalled them to start. At the first clash of steel, the other squires turned in surprise. They were quick, but they almost missed the action. In three or four seconds, Giles had forced the blue squire halfway back to the stables; a moment later, a sword flashed through the air and fell to the ground with a clank. It was all so fast that she couldn't tell what had happened until she saw Giles step back to allow his opponent to pick up his sword. They faced off again in silence; the other squires stood very still, and the knights who had been chatting by the stables watched closely. Giles and the blue squire circled each other, then Giles closed in, moving so fast that his sword became a blur of shining steel. In less than a minute, the blue squire's sword flew across the court-yard and landed at Sir Piers's feet. Smiling, Sir Piers picked it up, but instead of giving it back, he said something to both contestants and pointed to where the other squires stood.

Shoot! They were all moving towards the area past the blacksmith's shop – which made sense, since that's what it obviously was for, but she wouldn't be able to see beans from where she was. Just when Giles was going to get his chance, too! Well, she could go down to the courtyard . . . yeah, sure. And if she went down, followed them all the way out to the swordplay area, and one of the dogs who wasn't Malachi saw her, how could she possibly get away? Forget it. She'd just have to— No, wait! What about the parapet? If she went back up there, she could walk along the wall until she was right above them! She jumped down from the bench and hurried towards the stairs.

The door was shut. That was strange; Sir Piers had left it open, and she hadn't heard it slam or anything. Could somebody have closed it? Locked it? In sudden panic, she yanked on its handle – and slipped through, feeling silly, because it opened easily. It had just shut itself, and she'd been so engrossed, she hadn't—

She stopped, looking around in confusion. These weren't the right stairs. They were straight. They were made of wood. She was back in— No, no! She wouldn't let that happen! Turning round, she fumbled for the door's heavy latch. But there wasn't a latch. There wasn't even a door – nothing but the stairs, and they only went up. Biting her lip in frustration, she started to climb them. At the top was Con's attic, with a window to Aunt Joan's house right where it had been before. And at the far end of the attic, curled up on the old sofa, was Con.

10
Duets

It couldn't be spatial disorientation this time. She'd looked over her shoulder very carefully as she'd gone down those tower steps, and she'd known exactly what they'd look like going back. Obviously, they weren't the usual kind of steps, any more than the window was the usual kind of window. Whatever logic might be behind it was evidently the kind behind right and left, which meant, of course, that there was no way she could figure it out. Still, however weird this was, it was at least interesting. The best thing to do, probably, was just go along with it – though it was hard not to feel cheated about Giles and the swordplay. Not to mention embarrassing to keep interrupting Con's disappearing time, which was probably what she'd done. She shot a glance to the end of the attic. For sure. You didn't curl up like that if everything was fine. Well, the stairs could send her here, but they couldn't make her bother him. It was a shame to waste all those

Hink Pinks she'd been saving up in case she saw him again, but she should just go home and—

A board creaked under her foot; Con started and looked up. 'Erin!' He sat up, blinking. 'Champion Sneaker-Upper Strikes Again! No House in Upstate New York Safe from Random Visitor! What brings you here?'

It would never do to admit she had no idea; he'd just go on about that psychiatrist who lived three doors down. 'Well,' she said, 'you said to come back when I could, and this is when I could. Good thing, too – you look like you need cheering up.'

He looked at her defensively. 'What makes you say that?'

'I forgot to tell you: Champion Sneaker-Uppers have ESP – every single one. But only a few of them know how to play Hink Pink. You're in luck.'

'I'll be darned,' he said. 'I thought you didn't like it.'

'I changed my mind. What do you call the green stuff that grows on leftovers in the refrigerator if you leave them there too long?'

He thought a minute, then smiled. 'Cold mould!'

'Excellent,' she said. 'And if you have a bunch of sparrows sitting on a telephone wire, what you call number three in the line?'

'Give me a hint,' he said, frowning. 'Hink pink if it's one syllable, hinky pinky if it's two, and so on.'

Never mind telling him you couldn't read two-syllable words yet. 'Hink pink.'

'Drat,' he muttered. 'I just can't— Oh! Third bird! That's so clever, it suggests you're ready to graduate to Tom Swifties.'

'To what?'

'Same idea, different rules. You know how in books, you get lines like *"Look out," said Tom, urgently?* OK, what you do is make that tag into a pun, like this: *"I burned my tongue," said Tom, hotly.*'

She groaned.

'Groan away,' he said. 'The question is, can you think of one?'

Could she think of one? Little did he know she was always the one who could *never* . . . yeah, but this was like Hink Pink – you didn't have to see it; you could just listen. Maybe . . . Well, if you could say something hotly . . . Suddenly, out of nowhere, it came. 'What about *"I hate ice cream," he said, coldly.*'

' *"Very good," he said, tastefully.*' Con grinned. 'And it worked, too – I've cheered up. Wouldn't have thought it possible. Listen, want to complete the job by playing duets?'

She shook her head quickly. 'I can't . . . sight-read.'

'Who said anything about sight-reading? I mean *real* duets, like my father and I used to play. It's easy: you play a tune, and I make up an accompaniment.' He hurried towards the stairs, his face lit up with enthusiasm. 'Come on down, and I'll show you!'

Brother – what would happen to the stairs if she

went down them? 'Um, what about your mom? I mean . . . she doesn't know I'm here.'

'She's at some meeting – won't be home for hours.'

He started down; she followed slowly, holding her breath when he got to the place where the castle door had been. There was another door now, to the side. It *couldn't* have been there before – she'd have seen it! But he gave it the kind of shove that suggested he opened it all the time; and when she went through it, there was a normal hall. He led the way past six perfectly arranged bedrooms, down a handsome staircase with two landings, and into the big room where he had been practising last time she'd seen him. She glanced at the window she'd come through before; against the outline of the old trees outside, she saw the darkness of the little room at Aunt Joan's.

'Now, then!' said Con, slipping onto the piano bench nearest them. 'We'll begin on one piano so I can show you what to do. You sit at the treble, and – hey, is something wrong?'

'No, no,' she said, hurriedly sitting beside him. And there really wasn't, so long as she could get back. It was just spooky to have a window follow you around like that.

'OK,' he said. 'Let's try something simple. Can you play "Frère Jacques"?'

'I think so.' She tried it, and made it, more or less.

'Great,' he said. 'Only look: finger it this way, so you don't get tangled up.'

She made her hands do what his had done, and it worked. 'Hey, that's cool!'

'Fingering's *everything* when you're improvising,' he said. 'Or just playing, for that matter. My dad taught me that; he really knew. OK, let's try it together. You start.'

It sounded easy enough, but she got so distracted when he came in that she messed up right away. 'I'm sorry.'

'Don't stop, don't stop!' he said, going on. 'Even if you make mistakes, get yourself back on. That's the important thing. Start . . . again . . . *NOW*.'

She scrambled in, but the second she started paying attention to what he was doing, she messed up again. She managed to get back in with her right hand, but she couldn't get her left hand co-ordinated. If only he'd stop and pick up the pieces!

'Keep going!' he said, playing on relentlessly. 'Pick it up at the *ding-dongs*!'

By some miracle, that worked. And this time, she forced herself to listen *only* to what she was playing, not to him, and they played it all the way through. Twice.

'Fantastic!' he said, stopping at the end. 'You've got it! Most people — girls especially — get all flustered when they make mistakes, and you have to repeat it over and over . . . hopeless. But you're a natural.' His smile lit up his funny-looking face. 'Let's improvise a bit, huh? Do you know about fourths and bells? . . . OK, but you do know what a fourth is, right?'

'Um . . .' She felt herself freezing. 'It's . . . like, an interval. And on the staff—'

'Forget the staff,' he said impatiently. 'We're talking about *real* music, on the keyboard and in your head. Can you *play* a fourth?'

She thought of guessing, but that was like faking, and besides, if she was wrong, he'd laugh. Blushing, she shook her head.

'Hey,' he said, 'don't look like that. It's not *your* fault you've been taught by a teacher who's tied to the page. The world is lousy with them, and if your parents aren't musical, they think music is like reading, so they don't know any better.'

'Just a sec! Music *isn't* like reading?'

'Absolutely, totally *not*! Music's like *stories*. People sang songs and told stories for *centuries* before they wrote them down, and learning by ear was as normal as learning off the page is now. But people with lousy memories and bad ears invented writing so they'd look better, and then, of course, they took over because there were so many of them, and they made everyone else learn things their way. If you have a real ear, though, you don't have to put up with that kind of tyranny. Take fourths, for example. It's confusing to see them on a staff, right? But look at this.' He put his thumb on a C and his fourth finger on an F. 'OK, tell me how many white keys are being covered here, including the two my fingers are on.'

'Four . . . omigosh! Then a third is three white keys,

and a fifth is five, and so on, right up to an octave?'

'Well, it's a little more complicated than that – you have to figure in the black keys – but essentially, yeah.'

'And that's *all* there is to learning intervals?'

'Not if you're playing by ear; then you need to hear them in you head. But that's a piece of cake if you have perfect pitch. Fourths are good to start with, because every one of them sings, "Here Comes the Bride".' He played it, grinning. 'Try it.'

C, F-F-F . . . D, G-G-G . . . E, A-A-A . . . Amazing.

'Great!' he said. 'Now play those again, only playing both the notes in the fourth at the same time – good! Sounds like bells, right? Congratulations! You just improvised the first three notes of "Frère Jacques"!'

'I *did*?'

'Sure! Try the whole thing now, all in fourths. What you do is freeze your hand in "fourth" position and play the melody with your thumb. See how far you can get.'

She got as far as the end of '*sonnez les matines*', which he said was predictable. But after he'd showed her a couple of tricks, she more or less got it, at least with the right hand, and he began to do ding-dongs in fourths in the bass. It sounded a bit like the bell piece she liked so much, and it sent the same shivers down her back.

'Great, huh?' he said. 'And that's only the beginning! Let me switch to the other piano – there. Now, you play the ding-dongs, and I'll do fancy stuff.'

She did what he said, and . . . well, it was like last time. You hated him for showing off, but you couldn't help being impressed. He began with a whole bell-like scale, then launched into the 'Frère Jacques' in fourths with his right hand, and 'Pop Goes the Weasel' with his left. It sounded as if a whole church tower had gotten loose.

'That's awesome,' she said when they finished. 'I wish I could do fancy stuff, but my fingers don't know where to go.'

'You have to train them,' he said. 'And I bet that teacher of yours hasn't taught you how. Do you play scales and arpeggios?'

'Sure — scales, anyway.' And she played a C-major scale, just to show him.

He was less than impressed. 'That's only one octave! And only one hand! That won't get you very far. You gotta do them all the way up and down the piano.' He was off, roaring up the piano in C and down in C sharp, so fast it made her head spin . . . and then she realized it wasn't just her head. Something very strange was happening. Dizzily, she reached for the piano to balance herself, but what she touched was a window frame, and she was sitting on the sill, not the bench. Clinging to the frame, she stood up and looked back. There was Con, still playing, but he got dimmer and dimmer, and the sound of scales got further and further away, then disappeared all together. She was standing alone in the dark room, and the thunderstorm seemed to be over, because there was total silence.

No, not total silence. Somebody was padding down to the bathroom. She tiptoed across the room, opened the door, and stood behind it, listening anxiously to the toilet flush, the water run in the sink, the door open. Footsteps shuffled a couple of steps, paused . . . oh, no! But nothing happened. Just a sigh, then more footsteps. She waited until they were entirely gone, then snuck down the hall herself, starting at every creak in the floor, and crawled into bed.

11
A House Is Sold

When she woke up, her clock said 9:00. She rubbed her eyes, looked again, then picked up her watch from the night-stand. 9:01. Omigosh! Tumbling all over herself, she got dressed and raced downstairs without even making her bed.

'I'm sorry, Aunt Joan,' she began as she hurried into the dining room. 'I—'

But Aunt Joan wasn't there. Only Uncle Druce, looking up from his catalogue. 'Toast?'

'Um . . . sure.' She went to her place. 'I'm sorry I'm so late.'

The toaster popped up as she sat down; he handed her one piece and put the other on his plate. 'Saturday,' he said, putting in two more slices. 'No work; no routine. Breakfast anytime.'

He spread jam thickly on half his slice and peanut butter on the other half, folded it into a sandwich, and shoved the jars towards her. When the next pieces

121

popped up, he handed her one while turning a page. She munched away, drank the milk that had been at her place, and waited for him to look up. But he didn't. Not even after he'd finished. She squirmed as the minutes on her watch slid by. 9:20. 9:25. 9:30.

'Uncle Druce?' she said finally.

'I'm not your uncle,' he said without looking up. 'I'm your second cousin once removed. You know what that means?'

For once, she did. On the way home from the last Easter Family gathering, she and Rob had whiled away the time figuring cousins out. 'It means you're Mom's second cousin, which means her grandmother was your grandfather's sister.'

His examined her through the top of his bifocals, with an attention he usually paid only to bottle caps. 'Strange,' he said finally.

'What is?'

'Well, you don't *sound* like a halfwit. But you've been sitting there, doing nothing, for . . . what, a quarter of an hour?'

She felt her face go red. 'I was waiting to be excused!'

'For what?'

'Not *for* what – *from* the table. And I . . . I didn't want to interrupt!'

'Oh, yeah,' he said reflectively. 'The niceties of Family life. It's been a long time since I've thought about them. Sure, you're excused.'

'Thank you. Um . . . do you know where Aunt Joan is?'

'With the realtor. House just closed.'

'Excuse me?'

'Thought I just did that.'

'I meant . . . never mind.' Aunt Joan would explain it when she got home. 'Will it bother you if I play the piano?'

'Nope.' He went back to his catalogue, but he looked up quickly as she cleared their plates. 'You know, if you stack them like that, you'll have to wash the bottoms.'

She picked up one plate in each hand and took them to the kitchen. There really *was* something wrong with him. Not violent, or anything. But you never knew what to think about him. Like, if he'd been a normal person just now, you'd think he'd been laughing at her, and he'd been serious. At least . . . She wandered back into the dining room, thinking maybe she wouldn't play the piano after all. But he was gone.

She stared at his empty place, feeling guilty. *Did* the piano bother him? Or worse, had he known she didn't feel comfortable when he was around? Or had he just gone upstairs to get more bottle caps? She puttered around, brushing toast crumbs into her hand, washing his coffee cup and her milk glass, but after ten minutes, he still hadn't come back . . . *Funny, you don't* sound *like a halfwit.*

Suddenly, there it was in her mind: what *really* made

you a halfwit where Uncle Druce was concerned was thinking he cared about what you did. That was what made him so different from other people. He lived in a kind of bubble, and nothing outside that bubble mattered to him. Which meant . . . well, all sorts of things, but basically, you could play the piano all you wanted without bothering him.

She started by trying to work out 'Frère Jacques' as a round with herself, one hand playing each voice. It took so long that she decided against even trying it with both hands in fourths, but she did figure out how to do the impressive-sounding bell thing Con had done. You just played your way down a C-major scale with your hands frozen in fourths, and you could add booming bells in the bass. It was fun, and it sounded great on this wonderful piano . . . but she couldn't come anywhere near doing the neat things Con had done with it.

She gazed out the window, thinking about Con's fingers zipping around the keyboard, Sir Piers's fingers moving over his lute easily while he sang. Finger athletes, that's what they were. And anybody who knew Rob knew you couldn't become an athlete unless you trained and trained and trained. OK. So how did you play a scale all the way up and down the piano? She tried it a bunch of different ways, but she always came out with fingers left over at the top. That couldn't be right! There had to be a—

The back door opened and shut; a minute later,

Aunt Joan stumped into the dining room, looking hot and frazzled. 'Hello,' she said. 'D'you mind having lunch early? The old house has sold, and I have to go there this afternoon to settle a few details – no, no, go ahead and play. It'll be a half-hour before I'm organized. Scales, is it?'

'Yeah, but they're not coming out right. There's got to be a secret!'

'It's no secret, if you have a decent teacher,' said Aunt Joan tartly. 'There's a pattern.' She made scooting motions with her hands, and Erin slid over to make room for her on the bench. 'Start with both thumbs on middle C, like this, and go in opposite directions. Now, watch: one-two-three, cross the thumb under, one-two-three-four, cross the thumb under – and you're back to C. Now you try . . . atta girl! Now, keep working on it to make it a habit – stick with opposite directions at first, so the crossovers come at the same time.' She got up. 'I'll be gone all afternoon, and it's supposed to storm again. You want to go along with me, or stay here with Druce?'

'Oh – I'll go along with you,' said Erin quickly. No question.

When she thought of driving places, of course she thought of freeways, but Aunt Joan thought differently. All the roads they took were two-laners, and between the malls and supermarkets and gas stations outside of towns, there were pretty stretches of woods and farms and hills. Aunt Joan sighed as they drove past the first farm.

'When I was your age, sixty-odd years ago, it all looked like this,' she said. 'Glad I'm due to die before they pave over everything that's left.' She glanced to the side. 'Did Druce say anything about what's happening to the old house?'

'Just that you were selling it.'

'Yeah,' said Aunt Joan sadly. 'To a guy who's going to turn it into a B and B. Grandfather is spinning so hard in his grave, I bet we'll be able to hear him when we drive by the cemetery. He built the house for his wife, and in the eighteen-nineties it was the most beautiful and up-to-date place on Main Street. Even in the thirties, when I was growing up there, it was a land-mark, which is fortunate, in its way, because before Victorian houses became chic again, most of the houses on Main Street got torn down and replaced with banks and insurance companies and law offices. But nobody wants to live in the middle of banks and insurance companies and law offices, even in an old landmark. There was never any question of selling it to a family; a B and B is about the best we could hope for. I had nightmares about its being taken over by some computer company that would drill holes in the panelling and cover all those beautiful floors with institutional carpeting.'

'Couldn't you and Druce have gone to live there?'

Aunt Joan shook her head. 'It was a complicated

situation – not that there's anything else in the Family. But my branch was more complicated than most. My father married twice, and he had six children altogether: five with my mother – I'm the oldest – and Druce with my stepmother. He left the house to all of us, but he gave my stepmother the right to live in it for the rest of her life. She died last month, and the furniture was distributed according to his will – that's why the piano showed up the day after you came – but the house was divided "share and share alike", which means we each got a sixth of its worth.'

'That makes sense.'

'Yes, it does, financially. But you can't divide up the worth of a house the way you can divide an apple. The only way Druce and I could have lived there was to buy the rest of the house from the others, and we couldn't afford that. So it got sold.'

'The others didn't want to keep it?'

Aunt Joan snorted. 'Erin, since when has *anybody* in the Family cared about anything but money and success?'

Since when had anybody in the Family dared to say anything after an Aunt Joanism like that? Erin leaned her head back on the seat and looked out the window until the farms turned back to another strip. Gradually, her eyelids drooped. Staying up half the night made you awfully sleepy in the afternoon. But it was worth it. Sir Piers and Giles, Con and his scales . . . it was just . . . so . . .

'Erin?' Aunt Joan was smiling at her. 'Wake up, honey. We're here.'

She got out of the car, rubbing her eyes – then rubbed them again as she looked around. Behind her, a driveway wound up through huge trees. In front of her was the most beautiful house she'd ever seen. It was enormous – a mansion, really – but everything was the right size to go with everything else, so you didn't notice that right away. What you noticed was the 'everything': a circular tower on the side, big bay windows in the front, dormers built into the hipped roof, decorated with fancy trim . . . wow. No wonder Aunt Joan felt bad about selling it!

Wheels crunched on the driveway, and a classy black car pulled up next to Aunt Joan's rusting station wagon. The woman who got out looked like the other aunts in the Family – power suit, carefully placed neck scarf, beauty salon hair and nail job. She acted like them, too, shaking hands with both of them as she introduced herself ('Joyce Kildare, of Kildare and Wicket') and saying how glad she was to meet them. But as usual, that sort of thing was wasted on Aunt Joan.

'Here comes the storm they predicted,' she said, looking up as big drops began to fall. 'Let's get inside before we drown. Side door?'

'No, front,' said Mrs Kildare, taking a key out of her purse as she hurried up the steps. 'That front hall makes such an impression.'

It did, even though it was a bit dark with the rain and all. There was a handsome staircase to one side, and over the first landing was a huge window with coloured glass squares all around its edges. The hall had shoulder-high panelling, and on the wallpaper above it there were rectangular clean spaces where there had been mirrors or pictures. Even the floor was beautiful; instead of being laid out the dull, parallel way wood floors usually were, it was placed in squares, each board set inside the last until you got to the middle, under the chandelier, where there was a single piece of wood.

'Like it, Erin?' said Aunt Joan, sighing. 'So do I. Well, take a look around. Mrs Kildare and I have to talk about the wiring and the furnace – can't think you'd find it interesting.' She pointed to the big room off to the side of the hall. 'That was the music room; in its day, it was the musical centre of all Mohawk Valley. The piano that's at home now lived in there; it was one of two while our father was alive, and some years after, until my stepmother sold the other one. Through the double doors on the far side was the living room. And over here—' she started towards the door straight ahead of her – 'was the dining room, and beyond it, the kitchen. That's where we'll be – it's the only place with a table and chairs, now – unless we're in the cellar.'

She walked away with Mrs Kildare, their footsteps echoing through the empty rooms. Erin turned to the music room, wondering why a house without furniture in it, even a beautiful one like this, looked so sad. Maybe it was just thinking what it must have looked like when a musical family lived here. Chairs. Rugs. Instruments. They'd really make a difference. And of course, the pianos. You'd put them in the bay window, obviously, and in a room this size, you could open the lids and really . . .

Two pianos. In a bay window.

Come on. There were lots of houses with bay windows.

But not with two pianos. Not with a bay window at the end and three big ones along the side. Well, probably not. She walked slowly towards the bay window, stood where the pianos would have been, and looked at the other three windows. Nothing, of course. Just the raindrops sliding down them. But it was weird. Definitely weird.

She wandered back into the hall and looked up the handsome staircase. Aunt Joan hadn't said anything about not going upstairs. There was no reason she couldn't just go and check. She wound her way upwards, feeling peculiar every time she looked down, and even more peculiar as she walked down the long hall, counting the empty bedrooms. One, two, three, four, five, six. At the end was a closed door.

She put her hand on the knob, half hoping it wouldn't turn, but it did. And rising to its right (or was it left?) was a staircase. Switching on the light at the bottom, she climbed up . . . and there was no question about where she was, now. It was totally empty, but it had the same atticky smell, the same windows, the same nails coming through the roof. All that was missing was her window, back to Aunt Joan's.

She stood still, listening to the rain beat on the roof. It couldn't be real, what she was seeing. It was some kind of freaky disorientation nobody had ever heard of. Or . . . or . . . Something rustled in the dark corner farthest away from her. She froze, listening – then bolted down the steps and out into the hallway.

There was nothing, of course. Just a hallway with three bedrooms on each side, and at the far end of it, voices drifting up the stairs. Not weird voices, either: Mrs Kildare and Aunt Joan, then footsteps and Aunt Joan's voice alone, calling her. There was nothing in the music room when she got to the bottom of the stairs, either: only Mrs Kildare in a polite hurry to leave, and Aunt Joan, looking irritated. It didn't do to ask questions when grown-ups looked like that, so she said goodbye and scooted out to the car. But she couldn't help looking over her shoulder as they started down the driveway. The attic window looked out right over the circle in front of the house; there was plenty of room for a thousand-gallon vat of Roquefort dressing.

'Well, I'll tell you one thing,' said Aunt Joan, as she turned onto Main Street, 'the hassle of selling a house almost saves you from the pain of losing it. An hour and a half each way for a twenty-minute discussion over a fifty-dollar repair! You have to wonder what your time is worth.'

There wasn't much you could say when Aunt Joan got like that, so Erin nodded, looking out at the wet law offices and insurance companies, and wondering if she dared ask . . . No. It was impossible. She was just crazy, that was all.

'For heaven's sake, Erin! Can't you find anything to say?'

'I'm sorry. I was thinking about the house.'

'Suppose you tell me what you were thinking.'

'I was thinking how nice it was—'

'Well, that's good to hear.'

Erin drew a deep breath. 'And I was wondering . . . about your brothers and sisters. Was one of them named . . . um . . . Con?'

The car veered to the side as Aunt Joan jumped. She corrected it right away, but there was no doubting how surprised she looked. 'Yes . . . long ago. However could you have known that?'

'I just . . . well, I was trying to remember which of the aunts and uncles were your brothers and sisters, and I couldn't think of all of them. Then I remembered the Family had talked about somebody named Con, and I was wondering if he was one of them.' That wasn't faking; it was outright lying. But she would have plenty of time to feel guilty later. 'Um . . . did he play the piano?'

'Beautifully. Wonderfully.' Aunt Joan kept her eyes carefully focused on the road. 'We all played – our father was a professional pianist, and music was so

132

much a part of our lives that I must have been ten or so before I realized there were households that *weren't* musical. But Con was exceptional. I still think I hear him in the middle of the night, sometimes.' She sighed. 'What a tragedy – and so *unnecessary*. All that talent . . . just gone.'

Gone. What? The talent, or Con? And if it was Con, was he dead? Oh, no! He couldn't be! Not Con, with his dumb jokes and his word games! She looked at Aunt Joan, aching to know more, but she knew better than to ask. You didn't talk about tragedies in the Family; even if you were directly concerned, you hushed them up. So there was no way of knowing. On the other hand, maybe she didn't want to know. She leaned back in her seat, listening to the swish of the tyres on the wet pavement and the thump-thump of the wipers. The whole thing was weird enough without wondering if you'd been playing duets with a ghost.

12
A Siege Forestalled

At dinner, Aunt Joan told Uncle Druce about their afternoon; he listened, but as soon as she was finished, he went back to his catalogues. Aunt Joan didn't look surprised, but Erin wished he'd said just a few words; you didn't have to be a genius to see that selling the house had made Aunt Joan sad. Or that talking about Con had made her even sadder – though of course there was no way Uncle Druce could know that. She thought of saying something herself, but before she could figure out what, Aunt Joan opened the evening paper and they finished the meal in their usual way.

Except it wasn't their usual way; they were just doing their usual things, and not even those, really. When Uncle Druce went upstairs, he shambled more than usual, and instead of sitting down to read after dishes, Aunt Joan cleaned the stove and the counters and the shelves – slowly, painfully, but in a way that told you it would be smart to disappear. So Erin went up to the window seat in her room and sat there, feeling bad about Con, and thinking how terrible it would be if something happened to Rob and she could never see him again, and watching the grey sky get darker and darker. When the lights in the shabby houses across the street began to go on, she went to bed and cried herself to sleep.

She woke up needing to go to the bathroom so desperately that she'd gotten halfway there before she realized there was music somewhere, and not singing, either. Was it . . . ? Yes, it was. A piano. Which meant that whether she wanted to deal with a ghost or not, what was in the window was — Yeah, but she wouldn't have to go in. She could just go past, which she *really* needed to do anyway. She whizzed past the little room, closed the bathroom door, and — boy, not a minute too late. As she washed her hands, the piano started again . . . but was it a piano? How could she possibly not be able to tell? She crept into the hall, listening. It sounded like . . . like trumpets, way far away. And shouting, quite a bit closer. And the clank of armour. She peered around the doorjamb of the little room just in time to see the castle emerge from a swirling mist, huge and grey in the window. As soon as she could properly see the parapet, she realized something was going on. Everywhere she looked, men were working frantically, some carrying enormous vats, some assembling stones and others — knights and guards, mostly — pointing towards the plain and talking.

Obviously, this was not a good time for her to pay a visit, but if she got a little closer, she could see what was up. She inched into the room and climbed onto the sill, clinging to the frame cautiously – but not cautiously enough. As a knight whooshed by her, she lost her balance, and the next thing she knew, she was on the ramparts with everybody else.

She cowered against the wall, making herself as small as possible – luckily, it turned out, because the man who staggered by her with a load of wood would have knocked her over if she hadn't. After she'd dodged a group of kitchen boys carrying buckets and two men with more rocks, she learned that the big problem wasn't being seen or even sensed, but getting stepped on. Disappearing definitely had its disadvantages.

But it had its advantages, too; once she'd wormed her way to the place where the knights and guards were looking out over the battlements, she could hear them talk.

'The scouts should be coming back soon,' said the one in a red surcoat. Smiling, he added, 'You'll have no trouble guessing which of the squires wanted to ride with them.'

'No trouble at all,' said a knight in green, smiling too. 'Sir Roger's son is his father's image, and his reward will be knighthood at a tender age. Did you watch him in the lists last week? Seven lances broken, though it was only a practice – and every single squire unhorsed. His training is excellent, of course, but as with his swordplay, he has a sense of timing that can't be taught. If there is a siege, it will be hard to restrain him.'

'If there is a siege,' said the guard. 'It may be a false alarm.'

'That would be a shame,' said the knight in green. 'A little action would allow the squires to show their mettle without encountering much danger. If any castle can withstand a siege, it is this one, as Sir Piers well knows.' Shading his eyes with his hand, he looked around the castle walls. 'Where has he gone?'

The red knight smiled. 'To give the pages their singing lesson. Having organized all this—' he gestured about the parapet, where the men still worked – 'he decided that was the most fruitful way to while away the time. The boys have never stood a siege before, of course, and in showing them his lack of anxiety, he can offer two lessons in one – Ah, listen: they have begun.'

The others turned to the tower as the sound of soprano voices drifted wistfully through the sounds of scurrying footsteps, shouts and clanks on the ramparts.

> *'Lullay, lullay, litel child, child, lullay, lullow,*
> *Into uncouth world ycomen so art thou.'*

'And so they are,' muttered the knight in green, looking far, far over the ramparts. 'But I could wish Sir Piers had chosen a song with more cheer.'

The others nodded silently; as the plaintive song continued, Erin slipped along the wall, taking advantage of the sudden stillness that affected all the men who had been so busy up to that moment. Closing the tower door quietly behind her, she followed the voices down the spiral staircase to the familiar door. Malachi was pacing up and down in front of it, a crease of worry between his brown eyes. The crease deepened as he caught sight of her, and his lips curled in the beginning of a snarl. She stopped, extending a hand for him to sniff.

'Hey, Malachi,' she whispered. 'Remember me? I'm Erin. Your friend.'

He sniffed delicately, and the snarl became a dignified look of recognition that faded into un-easiness as something crashed upstairs on the ramparts. 'I know,' she whispered. 'There's an awful lot going on. It's enough to upset anyone.' She stroked his head, and to her surprise, he leaned against her.

She would happily have stayed there quite a while, patting him, but the moment the pages' song came to an end, he broke away and trotted through the door. Following him cautiously, she edged along the inside wall and saw William the page and five other boys about her age facing Sir Piers. It looked like a perfectly ordinary singing lesson, except the boys kept glancing uneasily at the windows, and Sir Piers was dressed in a light-coloured tunic almost entirely covered by a suit of chain mail.

'Very nicely sung,' said Sir Piers, putting down his lute. 'We'll keep that for the knighthood ceremony.

But by that time, you should also be able to sing in harmony, so let's work on intervals. Dan, John and Peter sing this C – good. Now, Luke, William and Geoffrey, sing a major third above that.' The voices came in with an E, a little out of tune at first, but adjusting themselves right away. Erin looked around for a blackboard with hateful lines and spaces on it, but there wasn't one. It was true, then. The castle was one of those wonderful ancient places Con had talked about, where everyone learned by ear. Well, if they could learn that way, so could she! Quietly passing Malachi, who was walking back to his old position in the doorway, she slipped behind the row of pages.

'Now, William, sing an A – thank you. John, a fifth above that?'

A great shout rose from the courtyard, distracting John, which gave her a chance to think of the piano keyboard and count up five white keys. When he sang, it was the note in her head. Hey, she could do it!

'Peter, a C – good. Now Geoffrey, a fourth above that.'

A fourth! 'Here Comes the Bride' – she sang an F before she thought, and Geoffrey, who was still looking towards the windows, chimed in.

Sir Piers raised his voice calmly as the noise in the courtyard increased. 'Hold that F, Geoffrey. William, a fifth below that, please.'

A fifth down – that was hard, and William sure wasn't any help; he was totally distracted. Just as Sir

Piers began to frown, Erin got the right note and sang it softly into the boy's ear. Automatically, he chimed in, but he was obviously listening only to the footsteps that were pounding up the stairs. Listening to them herself, Erin slipped into a corner, in case there should be action.

Within seconds there was action. A knot of men burst into the room – four guards in clanking armour, carrying tremendous battle-axes, two knights in chain mail, a lancer with a black spear, and several archers dressed in leather, with bows taller than themselves – all with hard faces keen with excitement.

'They'll be coming over the plain, my lord,' said a guard.

Sir Piers's eyebrows shot up. 'The plain? Are they mad?'

'Not mad,' said the lancer, glancing towards the doorway as lighter footsteps raced up the stairs. 'Confident in their strength. And justly. They are too far away to count, but the scouts say—'

The footsteps reached the landing, and Giles ran in, his eyes shining. 'Yes, they are too far away to count!' he panted. 'And that is their madness! They think we'll huddle down here, awaiting a siege. But if we go to meet them, my lord – now, before the sun sets – we can destroy them. A feint to the south will make them turn towards the marshes.'

The older men murmured disapprovingly, looking at each other, and Sir Piers frowned. 'Giles, you exceed your station. No one here is accustomed to consult squires in matters of strategy.'

'True.' Giles flushed and bowed. 'But if they did, they would send me out with the squires and lancers, lightly armed, to group with our backs towards the marshlands and tease the enemy. That would make their whole cavalry charge—'

'—Pinning your tiny force between them and the marsh,' said Sir Piers dryly.

'So they would think!' said Giles. 'But instead of charging back, we would flank to the sides, and the archers you had placed in the marshes would rise out of the tall grass and shoot – in no danger from the charge, for the ground will not hold an armed horse. *Then* you and your knights, who had been waiting a little way away – could charge their flanks and rear, driving them forward – do you see?'

'I do,' said Sir Piers thoughtfully. 'But I don't see how we could get archers to the marshlands without their being seen.' He glanced at the bowmen. 'What do you think?'

The oldest bowman stepped forward. 'They are still on the far side of the woods. If we moved quickly, we could reach the marsh before they see us. Given a half-hour, we can station ourselves along its length.' He looked down for a minute, then met Sir Piers's eyes. 'It's a strategy that would allow us to show that battles are not won by knights alone.' The other men nodded in agreement.

There was a little silence as Sir Piers looked at them, then at Giles. Finally he nodded. 'Very well,' he said. 'It's a bold plan. But it will work only if the scouts support your opinion that the enemy is some distance off—'

'Of course they will!' broke in Giles indignantly.

'No doubt,' said Sir Piers. 'But before I expose you – and the rest of my men – to such danger, I wish to speak to the men who have seen the army first-hand.'

He spoke mildly, but nobody, even Giles, argued. Quietly, he walked towards the door, and they followed him. When the door at the bottom of the stairs closed behind them, the noise in the courtyard hushed as if by magic.

The pages had followed, too, so Erin crept towards the bench, hoping she could see what was going on through the window. But she didn't dare to climb onto it this time. Stretched out along half its length was Sir Piers's sword, sheathed in a beautifully wrought scabbard. Lying next to it was the blue surcoat Sir Piers had been wearing the first night she'd seen him, together with his long blue cloak. Besides those lay an enormous pair of chain-mail gloves lined with leather – gauntlets, that's what they were called – and an open helmet with just a piece that covered your nose. Leaning against the bench was his shield, kite shaped and emblazoned with a lute and a deerhound. She shivered a little as she looked at it all. Beautiful, of course, but it meant business.

Footsteps dashed up the stairs. As they drew nearer, she slipped back to her corner, which was a good thing, because William and two older pages ran into the room.

'Are they going to do it?' panted one.

'Yes!' said William, picking up the gauntlets. 'That's why Sir Piers sent us up here – we're to arm him in the courtyard while he gives orders.'

The oldest page shook his head. 'Sir Piers is taking the advice of a *squire*?'

'Sir Piers takes all advice he thinks is good,' said William proudly. 'No matter who gives it. That's why my father sent me here to be a page. In a few years—'

The oldest page punched him on the arm. 'In a few years, he'll still be waiting for his armour, if it's left to you. Here.' He tossed the helmet and the surcoat to the second page, draped the cloak over William's arms, and hefted the shield and sword himself. 'March!' The others scuttled out of the room in front of him.

Erin waited until the door at the bottom of the tower slammed behind them, then she climbed on the bench. Her breath came fast as she looked down; the whole courtyard was filled with armed men and dozens of attendants. Along the stables, grooms caparisoned huge horses that stamped and sidled with excitement, and pages hurried to and fro with lances, swords, maces and brightly coloured shields. Nearby, squires in chain mail helped the knights into their armour, lifting heavy pieces, fastening buckles, adjusting helmets. On the opposite side of the arched gateway, over a hundred archers stood by the walls, dressed in green and brown and shifting their feet as they waited for the command to march. Near them, lancers in Sir Piers's blue were massing together, holding restless horses, and in the far corner, pikemen were busy putting an extra edge on their axes. As she watched, Giles hurried out from an arch in the arcade, a crimson surcoat over his suit of brightly shining mail. A page – it had to be William – slid through the crowd and followed him like a shadow, until he was finally sent on some errand.

Across the courtyard, Sir Piers was everywhere, his chain mail flashing as his blue cloak swirled around him. A word to the knights here, a conference with the oldest bowman there, a quick stoop to help a little page who'd tripped, a discussion with the lancers, an order to the pikemen, a steadying hand on a rearing warhorse – every time Erin looked away, she looked back to find him in a different place, until gradually, the knots of men grew more orderly, and the noise lessened. Finally, a groom led a huge bay horse to the mounting-block, and Sir Piers sprang into the saddle. Out of nowhere, Malachi slipped through the crowd and stood next to him. It appeared to be a signal, for as soon as he was mounted, the lancers mounted too.

William appeared again, leading a dappled grey horse. As he handed its reins to Giles, other pages and stableboys appeared with other horses for the other squires, who led them as close to the gate as the press of the crowd would allow. A trumpet sounded, and the portcullis rose. The bowmen marched out in lines of four, followed by the lancers. As the last of the lancers disappeared, Giles mounted and lifted a hand; a moment later, the squires rode out the gate in pairs, their horses snorting and plunging. The pikemen and the guards marched off next; as they did so, the knights in full armour clanked ponderously to a series of mounting-blocks, and the grooms led out one great, prancing warhorse after another for them to mount. Sir Piers moved his own horse closer to the gate; as they mounted, the knights grouped behind him. When the last knights had adjusted themselves in their saddles and fixed their lances in their sockets, Sir Piers raised his right hand, and they started forward.

It was beautiful, magnificent, wonderful. Erin stood as tall as she could, steadying herself by placing one hand on the window frame, so she could see more. But it didn't help. In fact, everything slowly faded until all she could see was a dull movement of colour and an occasional glint of steel – and not even that, finally. Everything turned into a dizzying sort of whirl, and when things steadied themselves again, the frame under her hand was wood, not stone, and the window in front of her looked out over a gravel driveway and handsome green lawn three storeys down.

She turned round, blinking as her eyes adjusted to

the dim light. Sure enough, it was Con's attic – and there was Con, getting up off the floor, looking down at something she couldn't see. After a moment, he sighed, turned away from it and started towards the steps. She looked at him critically. He didn't look like a ghost; he just looked the way people looked when you'd barged in on them when they were doing something they really liked. Nothing spooky about that. She checked for her window, and it was there. Well, then. 'Hi,' she said. 'What are you up to?'

Con jumped about a mile. 'Jeez! I wish you wouldn't just appear like that! I thought you were a ghost!' He looked at her grumpily. 'I suppose you heard the whole thing?'

'What whole thing?'

'Oh, my mom was just up here, and she – well, you know how I told you that the world was lousy with teachers who want you to learn music from the page, instead of the way they did it in the old days?'

'You bet I do! In fact, I just saw—' At the last minute, she remembered she couldn't possibly go on. Fortunately, he wasn't paying attention.

'OK, the problem is, my teacher is one of those. And this morning at my lesson we had a big fight about it.'

Erin's eyes opened wide. 'You had a fight with a *teacher*?'

'Don't looked so shocked,' he said, grinning. 'It wasn't a fist-fight – it was an argument, and not even that, really. I was just being very firm. But teachers have you over a barrel when it comes to being firm. Mr Roberts (that's his name) called my mom a little while ago, and he told her he couldn't keep teaching me if I thought the way I did.'

'Boy, talk about being firm! But you're not going to give in, are you?'

'I have to. That's what I meant when I asked if you had heard it all. My mom was up here, and she said – well, a lot of things. But one of them was that I couldn't play in the concerto contest without Mr Roberts on the second piano, so—'

'Wait a minute! A second piano?'

Con sighed impatiently. 'A concerto isn't just a fancy sonata – it's something you play with an orchestra. That's what the concerto contest is all about; the person who wins gets to play his concerto with the Mohawk Valley Symphony, and that's a big deal. But part of the contest is demonstrating that you can play when somebody else is playing – so your teacher (or whoever) plays the orchestra part on a second piano. That's one of the reasons we have two pianos; the contest is always here, and until he died, my dad was either a judge or one of the teachers who played second piano. But obviously he can't play second piano for me, so if Mr Roberts stays firm, I've got to go apologize. Right now.'

Erin considered. 'Well, that's really complicated, but it doesn't sound hopeless. Can you maybe say you're sorry you were rude—'

'I was *not* rude! I explained my position very politely.'

'I'm sure you did,' she said soothingly, 'but when you disagree with grown-ups, they assume you're being rude, whether you are or not. So if you apologize about being rude—'

'—He'll accept the apology very graciously and go on with the lecture he gave Mom over the phone, about how I need to concentrate on professional skills, practise harder, pay attention to the music on the page . . . you know.'

Erin frowned. 'I thought you said he thought you were a prodigy.'

'Oh, he does,' said Con quickly. 'It's just that he has certain ideas about what prodigies should be able to do, and I— Never mind. Everything will be fine.'

He didn't look as if everything would be fine. He looked like there was a lot he wasn't saying. But then, his teacher was angry with him, and his mother was upset – nobody said everything about things like that. 'Sure it will be,' she said. 'Just listen until it's over. It's not like you have to change your mind or anything. After all, you're the awesome pianist, not them.'

That was about as encouraging as she could be, but he didn't brighten up. 'Yeah,' he said, shuffling his big feet. 'Well, I'd better hop to it.' He started down the staircase.

It was awful to see him so miserable. One last try . . .

'OK – but listen. What do you call a piece of cooked bread that's wearing a sheet?'

He stopped halfway down, and when he turned round, he was sort of smiling. 'A toast ghost,' he said. 'Not bad. Come back soon, and we'll play some duets.' He shoved open the door, waved and disappeared.

She went back to her window and slipped through, yawning. It was good to be back . . . Wait a minute! Somebody was playing the piano. Was she back, or had she ended up somewhere else in Con's house? She looked behind her; there was nothing in the window. And in front of her . . . Slowly, her eyes adjusted to the darkness, and she saw the toy boxes, piles of books, a few blocks. She was back, then. Could Con possibly have followed her? That didn't seem likely, but—

She tiptoed out into the hall and started down the stairs. This really *was* spooky. Somebody was certainly playing the piano, but there was no light on in the living room. Everything was pitch dark, including the stairs . . . crunch – ouch! She clung to the banister, her heart pounding as she pulled two bottle caps out of her foot. Was the whole box about to go? What would happen if it—?

The playing stopped. In the living room, there was a little thump as whoever it was lowered the keyboard cover, then the sound of the bench moving back. If she was brave enough, she'd see who it was when he came out into the hall . . . wafted into the hall . . . toast ghost . . . She scooted up the stairs as fast as she could and ran for her bed. When she finally got there, she dove in headfirst and lay under the covers, shaking.

Downstairs, the hall floor creaked; then footsteps started up the stairs . . . down the hall . . .

She had just about stopped breathing when she heard the click of a door closing. Not a ghost, then. She swam out from under the covers, gasping for air. But who would be playing the piano at – she glanced at her clock – 2:30 in the morning? She sat up, looking out the perfectly ordinary window at the perfectly ordinary streetlight. And suddenly she remembered Aunt Joan in the car: *Thinking about him still wakes me up at night sometimes.*

You wouldn't think Aunt Joan was the kind of person who would wake up thinking of her little brother and wander around the house at night. But there it was. She lay down again, feeling sort of sad.

13
Soldering Irons

She woke up in the morning wondering what would happen next. The answer, for the better part of a week – even though she played Bach faithfully and practised intervals, scales and arpeggios until her hands were ready to drop off – was nothing. You'd think that a house with a magic window that led two places and a ghost that played the piano at night would be an interesting place to live, but in the daytime, it was . . . No, *dull* wasn't fair. You couldn't say that about a place where you could play a wonderful piano for hours and hours, and nobody interfered unless you got stuck and asked for help. *Ordinary*, then . . . No. Fair, but not right. No way was it ordinary to collect bottle caps, or spend all your time in your study counting them, or reading catalogues at meals. And you could hope it wasn't ordinary to have nobody to talk to who really listened or cared. *Lonely* – there it was. Of course, that sort of thing didn't matter as much when you got old, but it was too bad. If they'd taken Rob for a couple of months, he'd have talked to Uncle Druce about the catalogues and Aunt Joan about the paper, and gotten everybody doing something together instead of giving in to the silence the way they did. But they'd taken her, the expert disappearer. Well, she fit right in.

It could be a lot worse, of course; structured time still wasn't the order of the day, but there was kind of a routine now. First there was breakfast; then Uncle Druce left for work, and there was a reading lesson. At first, it had only taken ten minutes or so, but these days she seemed to be able to last for over an hour, even though all she was doing was saying all those Hink Pink words over and over while she wrote them down. Aunt Joan made a big deal of something other people hadn't paid much attention to: the fact that she made letters a different way every time she wrote them. Once Aunt Joan explained that was like playing scales with a different fingering every time, you could see how doing that would get in your way, so they'd gone through the alphabet letter by letter, until her hand knew which way to go at the beginning of each one. That made her writing look a lot better, but the big payoff came when she started to write *cat* or *pad*, or whatever, and her fingers knew the whole word, the way they knew chords on the piano. Somehow, having it in your fingers helped you see it as well as hear; she knew every single one of those words now, and she never got them mixed up with each other. Aunt Joan said that was great – and when Aunt Joan said something, you knew she meant it.

The reward for having got it was moving on to words with long vowels (the ones that sounded like the letter they were), so *mat* became *mate* and *tot* became *tote*. You could hear the difference easily, and it made sense that changing one letter in a word changed the way the whole thing sounded, just the way adding another note to a chord changed everything about it. *Seeing* the change – or at least seeing what word you ended up with after you'd made it – was a different matter. Contrary to what people had been yammering at you ever since first grade, sticking an *e* at the end of a three-letter word wasn't the only way to make that change in sound. You could also sneak a vowel into the middle, and it had the same effect. The result was you could start out with a word like *pan* – and make it either *pain* or *pane*, which sounded exactly the same but meant different things. A chord would never do that to you. But as Aunt Joan said, it was beyond the skills of beginning readers to fix all the arbitrary and unfair elements of the English language; all you could do was accept the way things were. And practise. So they practised.

She looked up at Aunt Joan as she turned *got* into *goat* on the green magnetic board. 'What's wrong with me? Other kids learn this stuff in second grade, and I—'

'Cut the self-pity,' said Aunt Joan, putting down her

coffee cup with a thump. 'You turned *man* into *main* and *got* into *goat* in the same lesson, which means you're transferring what we've been working on earlier into what you're learning now. If there were something wrong with you, you wouldn't be able to do that. See what you can do with *cot*.'

Erin switched the letters around. *Cote*. It should mean what you wore when it was cold, but she was pretty sure it hadn't looked like that yesterday. Maybe it was like *got* and *goat*. *Coat*. That looked better. And if you put one over a kayak, you got a boat coat – though how you spelled *boat* was anybody's guess. She made *bot* on the board. It should mean buying something, but it didn't mean anything. She rubbed the side of her nose. 'Do you have to have a three-letter word that means something to add the extra vowel to it?'

'A three-letter word that means something . . .' Aunt Joan looked at the board. 'Oh. No, we're talking about sounds, not sense. *Cot* means something, and so does *coat*. But that's just happenstance. *Lut* doesn't mean a thing, but when you add an *e*—'

'Oh, you get *lute*!' Erin's mind flew back to the castle, where Sir Piers was sitting on the bench with Malachi at his feet. Maybe a page was coming in for a lesson about now – that is, if the castle was still standing. But it had to be. The strategy Giles had thought up had been so nifty. Even Sir Piers had thought so . . .

Aunt Joan tapped her hand. 'What's wrong with you is *not* Attention Deficit Disorder,' she said sharply. 'And you're too young for Alzheimer's. If you don't pay attention, it's your own fault. Let me teach you some tricky ones. Make *rut*.'

Erin fished out the letters, feeling her cheeks go hot. 'OK.'

'Now, put an *o* in front of the *u*. Thank you. You would think that was route, as in Route Nine. But it isn't. Put your hand over the *r*. What do you get?'

Erin frowned at it. '*Out*.'

'All right, take your hand off that *r*, and you get a disorderly retreat, which is—'

'A rout.' Just like Sir Piers's enemies would have been routed. If she could only get back to the castle, she could find out what had happened!

'I don't know where your mind is, Erin,' said Aunt Joan, shaking her head, 'but it seems to have left the table. So why don't you leave with it? We need bread and milk for lunch; will you ride down to the grocery store and get it, please?'

She couldn't mean that. She just couldn't. 'I . . . I don't know where the store is.'

'You will, if you can pay attention long enough to take directions. Go out on the street and turn left towards town – No, don't freeze. You know which way it is. Point.'

Erin faced the street and pointed away from the park.

'Very good,' said Aunt Joan. 'Now, does the hand you're pointing with play the bass or the treble?'

155

'Bass.'

'OK, for left, read bass throughout,' said Aunt Joan. 'Follow our street for five blocks, until you get to State Street. Turn left – bass – and go two blocks. The grocery store will be on the corner of your treble-hand side, right next to the hardware store.' She opened her purse and took out ten dollars. 'If you see some ice cream that looks good, pick that up too, OK?'

'Sure.' Nothing scary about it. Ha, ha. She had only been putting off looking for soldering irons for days because she was so sure she'd get lost if she went downtown.

'Fine. Now, repeat the instructions.'

'Um, I turn bass on our street, and go . . . a few blocks and . . .'

'You're lost already,' said Aunt Joan witheringly, 'and you haven't even started. Repeat after me.'

She did repeat it. Six times, which was what it took to get it exactly. She went out the door, repeating it, and she got the bike out of the garage, repeating it. Everything was fine, until she found there was a stop light at State Street instead of the usual stop signs, which was so distracting she forgot which way to turn. She was still trying to remember when the light changed, and the car behind her honked. Left – no, bass! She turned bass as fast as she could and pulled up next to the sidewalk, willing herself to stop wanting Mom. If Sir Piers could conduct a singing class when his castle was facing a siege, if those pages could sing their intervals even though they were scared to death, she could ride a bike in traffic. She took a deep breath, pushed off, and rode two blocks, looking to her treble side. There it was – next to a hardware store, just like Aunt Joan had said.

She bumped the bike up on the sidewalk by the hardware store, which had irons in the window under a big red sign . . . SALE. She stared at it. She could *read* it. It actually made a word go off in her head. She looked up and down the street; there were signs in other windows, too, and if she concentrated, she could read some of the words on them, too: OFF, SAVE, NOW, BUY. And back in the window next to her: SALE.

She was so busy staring at the word that it took her a minute to realize it was the irons that were on sale. She locked the bike to a parking meter and studied them. It was hard to tell how you would use them to put knights back together again. You couldn't just press. Obviously, you had to do something else, too. Maybe the man in the store would know. She went in and strolled up and down the aisle of irons, wishing she didn't break out in goosebumps when she walked into air-conditioned buildings, and trying to look grown up.

'May I help you?' said the man behind the counter.

It had worked! 'Yes, please. I'd like to buy a solder-ing iron.'

The man's polite smile became a real one. 'You

won't find it there. It's with tools, in the back. Would you like me to show you?'

'That would be very kind of you.' Was that what you said?

She followed him back through measuring tapes and light bulbs and switches to hammers, saws and wrenches. At the end of the aisle, he lifted something off a hook and handed it to her. It looked like a long screwdriver, except it had a cord coming out of its handle and a point instead of the thing that turned the screws. She looked up at him.

'Um . . . I thought . . . but I needed an iron.'

The man looked like he was trying not to laugh. 'Maybe you'd better tell me what you want to do with it.'

'Well, there are some lead soldiers that are broken, and I was going to glue them, but my uncle said even epoxy wouldn't work – I needed a soldering iron.'

'Your uncle was right,' said the man. 'And this is a soldering iron. What it does, see, is heat up. Then you touch it to solder—' he pointed to a coil of wire-like stuff – 'until it melts, and you drip the melted solder onto the soldier and stick his legs back on, or whatever.'

It made a lot more sense than what she'd been thinking. 'Thank you. How much does it cost?'

The man frowned. 'Honey, this isn't a tool I like to sell to a kid without her parents' permission. Hot solder can really burn you if you do things wrong, and if you put down the iron on the piece of paper you've got underneath whatever you're soldering, you're in trouble. Do you take my point?'

She did. Especially because she knew she wasn't going to be able to read the directions. 'Yes, but that's going to be a problem. My parents are in Paris; I'm staying with Aunt Joan . . .' Oh no, she'd forgotten Aunt Joan's last name. If she had ever known it. 'Um . . . on Wells Street.'

'Wells Street,' muttered the man. Suddenly his face lit up. 'Oh, is that Joan Zagajewski? The one with the school?'

Boy, she was looking dumber every moment. 'Well, she said the bike I'm riding now was the one she rode to school every day, and I know she was a teacher.'

'That's Joan Zagajewski, OK. But let me tell you, she was a lot more than a teacher. She and her husband founded that school, and ran it for more than thirty years. Surprised you don't know that – the place is still running, and it's real famous, even in the city. Up until they founded it, kids like my son got passed from one class to another, and all the teachers said they were too dumb to read. But Joan and her old man – Jan, his name was; we all called him Johnny – they took those kids who couldn't tell *God* from *dog* and found a way to make them learn. Not just reading, either. Johnny said that if the Lord took away with one hand, he gave double with the other, and the school's job was to find where that double was. It was computers with my boy, and now he makes four times what I make – big house, fancy car, the works.' He smiled. 'Well, you give your aunt my regards, and tell her I'll give her or Druce a soldering iron, and a whole mess of solder, anytime – but they gotta come and get it.'

'Wow!' Maybe there was a way she could tell Uncle Druce . . . well, she'd have to think about that later. 'Thank you very much.' She started down the aisle.

'Hey, listen!' he said, going back to the counter. 'If you don't know about that school, you really should go take a look. I mean, it's your family and all.' He got a piece of paper and began to draw a map. 'You're here, where the X is, see? Now, you follow State Street two more blocks, then hang a left—' he drew an arrow – 'then when that road Ts, go right, then left as soon as you can. That's it. It was the old mill – dead for years, of course – and rather than take it down, Joan had it cleaned up. We thought she was crazy, but she went her own way. That's what she does about everything – more power to her, I say. And you gotta admit, a few flowers, trees, you'd never know the old place for what it was.' He handed her the piece of paper. 'There you go.'

'Thank you,' she said, putting it in her back pocket. 'Goodbye.'

The man waved. 'Have a good one.'

Erin walked down the hot sidewalk and shoved open the door of the grocery store. Inside, it was almost like being back in the city. The place was just a hole in the wall, with shelves and shelves of cans, bottles, candy, potato chips and other things you weren't supposed to eat jumbled in together with big box-office movies you weren't supposed to rent. The difference was that Rob wasn't there to take care of the details, like what it was Aunt Joan had sent her here to buy. She looked at the crowded aisles, hoping for inspiration. Bread. That was right. And there was the kind of round bread Mom bought sitting right on the counter. Yeah, but Aunt Joan and Uncle Druce liked the soft stuff that came in plastic bags. That was across the aisle from the cooler, and by the time she'd selected the flabbiest bread she could find, she remembered about the milk and ice cream. But people in stores didn't understand that you just wanted milk and ice cream. They wanted to give you a choice: blue caps, green caps and . . . red caps. That's what she'd been drinking. As for ice cream, even she knew the little pints of Ben & Jerry's were expensive, so she got a big box with an enormous mountain of chocolate ice cream on it. She carried the whole works to the counter, gave the bored kid at the cash register the ten, and stuck the change in her pocket, feeling proud of herself. Groceries and a soldering iron all in one trip. It wasn't a big deal or anything, but she'd done the job.

As she loaded the bag carefully into one of the bike baskets, she looked up again at the SALE sign in the hardware store, just to be sure it still set off a word in her mind. It did, but looking was a mistake. The hardware man was standing out in the doorway, smoking. 'Second left, right at the T, first left – don't forget.'

Shoot. If she started home, it would be like telling him she didn't care he was nice. She smiled, sighed, and pushed off the way he'd pointed. After two blocks, she looked back, hoping he'd gone inside. But he'd actually moved down into the street to watch, and was pointing . . . bass. All right, all right. She looked carefully for traffic, then waved at him as she turned. The street went downhill, and there weren't any stop signs, so it didn't take long to get to the T. What he hadn't said was that the reason for the T was a river – well, he'd said the school had been a mill. If she'd been smarter, she would have put two and two together; being her, she couldn't even remember which way to turn. Maybe she should go back; he'd probably finished that cigarette by now.

On the other hand, it was pretty here. There was a park along the river with trees and flowers and things, just like he'd said, and off in front of her and just to the bass side, there was one of those big brick buildings you knew was either a factory, a prison, or a school. If that was it, it'd be dumb to turn back now. She pedalled slowly towards it until she came to a little street that led past the building's entrance gate to a waterfall. Cool. She rode to the fenced overlook beyond the gate and stood there, one foot on each side of her bike, looking. If you went to school here, what

162

you'd do at recess (if they let you) was throw sticks into the smooth water at the top and watch them pitch over the edge. Though come to think of it, that would be tough on the sticks.

She watched, sort of hypnotized, wondering what the school was like. If it was for people who turned words around, it had to be for kids like her. And if the hardware store man's son had graduated from it, some of those kids had obviously survived. More than survived, if their parents were proud of them. She glanced through the entrance gate at the building. There were geraniums in big buckets on both sides of the double doors, and boxes of flowers on the sills of all its windows. If you were inside, learning silent *es* or whatever, you'd see those flowers, and you'd always hear the waterfall, not cars, or trucks, or sirens. You had to wonder why nobody in the Family had said anything about the school, if it was famous even in the city. Usually, when somebody did something famous, or married somebody famous, everybody in the Family was very proud, but she couldn't remember hearing anyone mention a Jan, or even a Johnny. As for Zagajewski, she'd certainly have remembered that if she'd heard it, because it wasn't the kind of name people in the Family had. Westford, Harding, Bancroft . . . Omigosh! The ice cream!

Circling the bike around, she pushed off and rode back up the hill, which, like most hills, was steeper going up than coming down. She got a kind of panicky feeling as she got nearer to State Street, but she could see the hardware store from the corner, so she knew which way to turn, and Wells Street was the only one with a stop light, so she knew where to turn there, too. Back in one piece, and she hadn't gotten lost once. She stuck the bike in the garage, hauled out the bag, and started for the back steps, stopping as Aunt Joan's voice floated out the window.

'. . . And you should have *heard* her when I told her Erin was out on her bike! I thought she was going to call the local cops long distance from Paris, and get them to arrest me for neglect! And *this*, after she'd spent *twenty minutes* grilling me about "Erin's progress"! Jesus, Mary and Joseph! Never mind the scales she's figured out on the piano! Never mind the way she's teaching herself technique! Never mind that she's gritted her teeth and worked her way into a reading vocabulary of two or three hundred words in just three weeks! The only acceptable progress is fifth-grade reading level on the tests – preferably by magic, but certainly by September. And you asked why I insisted on taking the poor child for the whole summer!'

There was a murmuring sound – probably Uncle Druce trying to get off the hook.

'Right – and a good thing, too! What she called about – *ostensibly* – was that Herb's company *did* ask him to stay in Paris for another month. He said they might. *She* didn't, of course – couldn't face up to the

164

guilt of admitting it would be a relief to have eight whole weeks off after a year of sacrificing herself to a programme of constant, ineffectual interference. Poor thing – you can hardly blame her. Facing your maternal inadequacies must be draining if watching your firstborn turn himself into a one hundred per cent normal, charming, tone-deaf success has allowed you to think you were a good mother.'

She paused for breath, and there was another murmur, but of course it didn't have any effect.

'Ditch the losers! It's in the best Family tradition. Deny every sign of trouble, hover over every talent, applaud yourself as a nurturer, and when it fails, erase—'

'Joan!'

She stopped. *Uncle Druce*, of all people, had gotten her to stop. But that didn't mean it was safe to go in. *Ditch the losers*. Erin felt the ice-cream box squish against her ribs. Ditch the losers. It wasn't true! She was a loser, all right, but Mom and Dad hadn't ditched her! Everyone said how supportive they were – there was the psychologist, the camp she'd been supposed to go to, all those visits to the principal. It was dumb to get upset by Aunt Joanisms; there was never anything to them.

Not usually, anyway.

But nobody had said anything about maybe staying in Paris for another month. They'd just said Aunt Joan wanted her to stay as long as she would have stayed at the camp. There was a perfectly good reason for that, though; they'd only found out about Dad's business today, and Mom hadn't wanted her to worry about things that might not happen. Sure. It was like not telling you you were going to the circus until right beforehand, so you wouldn't get upset if something came up . . .

The back door opened, and Uncle Druce looked out. 'Thought I saw you wheel that bike by,' he said. 'Did you get ice cream?'

'Yeah.'

'Great. We'll have some for lunch.'

He shambled back in. She followed him, carefully not looking at Aunt Joan as she put the things on the table.

'Milk, bread, ice cream . . .' Aunt Joan's voice had that plastic sound people's voices got when they were upset and pretending not to be. 'Good work.'

'Thank you,' she whispered. 'Here's the change.' She pulled it out of her pocket, and the receipt with it. As she put everything on the table, she saw the hardware store man's map and remembered all the questions she'd been going to ask Aunt Joan about the school. But she didn't feel much like asking them now.

14
Condescension

During lunch, absolutely the only sound was chewing. There wasn't even the whisper of pages turning, because Uncle Druce and Aunt Joan weren't reading. After they'd eaten their ice cream, Aunt Joan cleared her throat and said that Mom had called to explain that they would be staying in Paris for another month because of Dad's business. Erin said that would be fine – like, what else could she say? Aunt Joan nodded and took the plates to the kitchen. Uncle Druce shambled upstairs. And Erin went to the piano.

Once you'd learned the patterns of scales, and you were just working on playing them fast, ideas drifted into your head while you were practising. Usually, that was sort of nice, but this time what drifted into her head, right in time with her fingers, was: *Ditch the losers!* She tried to shake it away, but all that got her was: *Deny every sign of trouble, hover over every talent . . . and when it fails, erase—*

167

Her fingers stumbled, but she corrected them fiercely instead of letting them stop. Erase what? Or, better question, Erase who? What had happened to Con? *So unnecessary*, Aunt Joan had said. *Had* he died? Or was he just somebody that had disappeared from the Family? What about Johnny Zagajewski? How come he'd disappeared? Was he a tragedy? What did it take to get you erased?

What would happen if she couldn't get to fifth-grade reading level by September? Her fingers stumbled so badly that she had to go back to the beginning of A major and start all over again.

Nothing. Mom and Dad would keep loving her, wouldn't they? All those things Aunt Joan said about Mom were totally unfair. Mom wouldn't let her be a tragedy. That was *why* the psychologist, the camp . . . that was why she was here, for heaven's sake! She switched to E major and made her fingers march up and down the piano. She *was* making progress. Aunt Joan had said so, and whatever you might think about Aunt Joan, she never lied. And she knew how to teach people to read. There was nothing to worry about, except, maybe, that Aunt Joan and Mom didn't get along. But if she could get into sixth grade, even that wouldn't matter.

She finished the scales and went on to the pieces she was trying to work out, but none of them sounded right, even the Bach hymn to piano-tuning, which she usually played pretty well these days. It wasn't the piece; it wasn't even the way she played it. It was the nasty little thoughts that kept snickering in her ears that wrecked it. It just wasn't fair to a beautiful piece of music to play it when you couldn't concentrate, so she quit and wandered upstairs past Uncle Druce's study to the little room.

There was nothing in the window, of course. Even when she walked right up to it, all she could see was Aunt Joan out in the back yard, looking at the over-grown beds of flowers. You had to wonder why she didn't do anything about them. There were those beautiful flowers around the school and its park, but here, nobody had pulled a weed for like . . . No, there she went. Slowly, slowly, she lowered herself on one knee and reached for a clump of grass. Well, at that rate, she wasn't going to have much—

She took a step backward, blinking. The garden, Aunt Joan, the colours were all going grey, and then – was it really? Very hard to tell, in the daylight. It could just be a reflection or a fog . . . Oh, wonderful, it wasn't! It was the castle.

She didn't realize the ramparts weren't fully in focus yet until she jumped onto them, but there was only a little squish before they got solid. She looked down at her feet as she moved from place to place; next time she'd be a bit more careful. Meantime, everything seemed to be just fine. The same guards on the towers, the same busyness in the courtyard, the same— No, wait, it wasn't the same out in front. There was a big

169

fence, like a stockade around an area close to the size of the courtyard. Behind it was another fence, and beyond that there was something that looked for all the world like a grandstand. Then in the middle there was a sort of low fence a hundred feet long, but it didn't fence anything in. She put her chin on the battlement in front of her, frowning as she tried to figure it out.

Behind her, she heard a scuffle of footsteps; turning, she saw William and one of the older pages. She expected them to go right by, but they stopped so near where she was, she moved over a couple of battlements. Just as well – they weren't any better at standing still than the boys in school, and they kept elbowing each other just the same way. You'd think working for Sir Piers would have a better effect on you.

'Look!' shouted William. 'Here they come!'

Erin looked across the plain at the woods for all she was worth, but nothing rode out of the trees. Were her eyes going, or— Oh. She looked down as hoofbeats clopped over the drawbridge. Warhorses! No wonder the boys were jumping up and down; she'd be doing it, too, if she weren't too mature. They were in full armour, prancing, snorting and skittering sideways. Controlling them – just barely – were squires on unarmoured cobs, while the knights looked after their painted lances and shields . . . shields. One of them was blazoned with a lute and a hound – Sir Piers! And the other?

'Poor Giles,' said the older page. 'I wouldn't want to be the first squire to joust with Sir Piers, even with hollow lances. There's not a knight in the whole country he hasn't unhorsed.'

'Giles *asked* to go first,' said William scornfully. '*He's* not afraid to be unhorsed; he says his father knocked him off two or three times a week, just to remind him how much he had to learn. You wait – he'll unhorse a lot of people at the tournament next week.'

A tournament. Of course! That's what they had built – lists! Boy, if she could only figure a way to get there to watch that tournament!

'Pooh!' said the older page. 'He just thinks he's the flower of chivalry because his little strategy worked out.'

'It wasn't a *little* strategy – it was a stroke of genius. I heard Sir Walter telling Sir Geoffrey that while I was serving dinner.'

'Some day, one of the knights is going to catch you listening, and you won't be able to sit down for a month,' said the older page. 'But – look! They're almost ready!'

At opposite ends of the stockade, the squires held the warhorses steady as the riders closed their visors and adjusted their shields, lances and reins. Then the cobs stepped away, and the two horses pranced towards the ends of the lists. For a moment, they paused, their fetlocks flashing as they stamped and snorted. The squire off to one side dropped a handkerchief. As it fluttered to the ground, both horses plunged into a canter and thundered towards each other. As they neared the centre of the list, the knights leaned forward; at the last possible moment, each of them raised his lance just a trifle . . .

CRASH! It sounded like a car accident, but it didn't look like one, because the horses went on. Both of them. With riders. The only thing that had changed was the lances. They were both in pieces.

A shout went up from both towers; looking up, Erin saw that several knights had joined the guards. Down on the ramparts, William did a little dance of joy. 'Two lances broken! He did it! He stayed in the saddle!'

'That's nothing unusual,' said the older page scornfully. 'Sir Piers often lets squires break a lance or two, to give them confidence before their first big tournament.'

William made some indignant remark, but Erin lost it; the ramparts were going squishy again, and next to her, *her* window grew larger and larger. No. She was not going to let this happen! She wanted to *stay* here for once, and see the end of things. She dashed towards the tower and yanked open the door. There! Now the window couldn't—

Oh yes it could. The stairs she was going down weren't the tower stairs. They were attic stairs. And at the bottom, the door went off to the side. She opened it a crack and peered around it. It led into the hall of Con's house, just like she'd thought. But there wasn't a sound anywhere. She turned round. 'Con?'

Nothing. Then all of a sudden, a piano. Downstairs.

She slipped along the long hall and started down the stairs. There he was, sitting at the piano nearest the window. And three windows down from him was *her* window, just the way it had been before. This time, though, he wasn't playing; he was listening to another piano play something with an orchestra, and his stereo was sprawled out on the floor. It sure was hard to carry music around back in his day, whenever it was! It must have taken five or six trips. So why . . . ?

He looked up and saw her. 'Oh, hello. What are you doing here?'

'Sneaking up. Want to play some duets?'

He got up and took the needle off the record. 'Not until I'm done here. But if you want to help, you could work this thing. It's hard to listen and play both.'

'So why are you doing it?'

He sighed. 'You know how I told you I had to go apologize to my teacher? Well, I did that, but of course it wasn't enough; I had to promise to reform. It seems I was improvising little bits of my Mozart concerto instead of playing what Mozart wrote, and he wants me to have it all worked out by the time of my lesson this week. So that's what I'm doing – and you're just the person to help me. See, what you do is put the needle down right about . . . here.' He set it down and the pianist on the record started into a really difficult run. 'Then, when he gets to the end, you take it off, and I play it, and you tell me if I'm playing the same thing. When I get it right, we play duets. OK?'

It was hardly a welcome, but it might be kind of interesting. 'OK.'

'Thanks.' He sat down at the piano. 'Charge!'

She lifted the arm carefully (fortunately, her dad had been *very strict* about how you lowered needles onto his old record collection) and set it down where he had shown her. It was just about right – the pianist charged into the run again. When he nodded, she took it off, and he played. That was right. That was. That—

'No, you went off just after the C sharp. Want it again?'

He grumbled something that was probably 'Yes.' Once more. This time he almost made it. 'That's close, but you added a few notes at the end. Wouldn't that screw up an orchestra?'

'They'd wait.'

'How could they? There are more of them than there are of you.'

He sighed. 'OK, OK. The trouble is, I've played it wrong so often that my fingers have learned it that way, and they don't want to change.'

'Why don't you look at the music?'

'This is faster – let's try it again.'

She put on the famous passage, wishing she could slow it down for him. This time, halfway through, he started playing along with the record, and he made it all the way through. 'Way to go!' she said.

He nodded. 'Take it off, and let me try it again.'

He played it through five times, then looked at her with a smile. 'Thanks a lot. There's more, but let's play a duet or two first. This kind of stuff kills me!'

She looked at the open music books on the rack. Some places were circled in pencil. 'Are you sure it's faster finding all those spots on the record than it would be just figuring it out from the page? Not that I could do it, but—'

'—But I can,' he said defensively. 'I just prefer it this way. It stays in my head longer. Now, about those duets. Have you been practising?'

'Yeah,' she said, sitting down at the vacant piano. 'Listen.' First she played the impressive bell scale he had played for her last time. When she got to the bottom, she switched into a C-major scale going up and a G major going down. Both hands.

He nodded judiciously. 'Not bad, for somebody who could only play one octave, one hand, a couple of weeks ago. See if you can play that bell scale while I play something else.'

Darn right, she could. He should be nicer than that! She started into it – and lost it completely as he started making it sound like Tchaikovsky. 'Whoa! Let's start again!' But of course that wasn't allowed; he just grinned and said, in time to the music, 'Get – back – in – NOW.' 'In' seemed to be the beginning, so, grinding her teeth, she started all over again, and this time she made it to the big bongs at the bottom. When she started playing those, he started playing 'Frère Jacques'.

Now she could show him! When it came time for the second voice, she swung into it, first with her right hand, and then with her left on a third voice. In answer, he came in with the fourth voice, in fourths.

'Hey!' he said when they finished. 'You *have* been practising, haven't you! Too bad we can't go on.'

'You mean we can't?'

'Nope. I have to get the rest of this concerto under my fingers. No time for goofing around. But you can be record boy if you want.'

She tried not to look as put off as she felt. 'How many passages are there?'

He shrugged. 'I don't know. Ten, twelve.'

'And you want me to stick around and put them *all* on for you?'

'If you want to stick around, that's what you've got to do, because that's what I've got to do.' He flipped grumpily at the music in front of him. 'The next passage should be about a quarter inch further in on the record – it's the passage leading into the cadenza.'

He was being a total jerk, but as she opened up her mouth to say so, she suddenly remembered Aunt Joan, wandering around the house at night. *What happened to you, Con? Why did you disappear? How come you were a tragedy?* She could *feel* something was wrong – there was something he was afraid of, and it sure as heck wasn't his teacher. Or his mom. It was whatever he was afraid of that made him so awful. Even Rob got that way before important tennis matches. And any good sister knew what to do.

She picked up the needle arm and set it gently on the record.

'No! That's the wrong place. A quarter of an inch *in*!'

'I *put it* a quarter of an inch in!'

'Well, farther, then!'

She bit her tongue and tried again. This time, he jumped up impatiently. 'Here – let *me* do it!'

She put the needle arm in its rest. 'Look – *nobody* can do this! It just takes too long to find little passages in a whole record! Either you should listen to it all the way through, very carefully, or you should get your music and—'

'Thank you,' he said in a voice that dripped acid. 'Little Error, who plays so sweetly for Mom and Dad's guests, has taken to giving lessons. I'm so *grateful*.'

She jumped to her feet. 'OK,' she said, choking back tears. 'I told you if you called me that, I was leaving, and I am. "*Good luck,*" *she said, charmingly.*'

Three steps, and she was at her window; two more, and she was back in the little room at Aunt Joan's. Looking back, she expected to see him hunting for her, or at least looking surprised – and serve him right! But he was just sitting in front of his stereo, lowering the needle.

Darn him! He didn't even care! The only person around here she could count on to cheer her up, and he didn't even care! She raced out of the little room, slamming the door so hard that she woke Uncle Druce, who had been snoozing in his tattered recliner.

15
A Squire Is Knighted

Somehow, knowing Con didn't care took the heart out of her. That was stupid; it wasn't like she knew him well or anything. She hadn't even realized he was important to her. He must have been, though, because after she'd zipped back through her window, everything that had been getting sort of interesting looked dull and dreary. Aunt Joan brought out an easy reader – typed and mimeographed, would you believe – so she could practise reading aloud. She could do it without faking, which should have been encouraging. But while she was trying to put expression and emphasis into sentences like *Bob is a slob. He walks in a blob of ink. His dad is mad. His mom is sad. They send him to his room,* what she was saying got drowned out by a little voice that snickered: *These are second-grade words. They aren't fifth-grade words. If you keep reading like this, even without faking, you will be stuck in fifth grade for the rest of your life. And then what will happen?*

On the third day of this, Aunt Joan put down her coffee cup with a thump. 'Erin, what's the matter?'

She wasn't angry; she really wanted to know. But what could you say? 'Nothing.'

'You do know how well you're doing, don't you?'

Not well enough, sniggled the little voice. 'Sure.'

Aunt Joan didn't look fooled, but she didn't say anything more, and after a while it was time for a bike ride, and that was that for the day. Except the voice kept up. Not the voice that told her she was going to get lost every time she turned a corner; that had disappeared about the time she'd started pretending Malachi was loping alongside her every time she went out. This was another voice, and it was like Aunt Joan: you never knew what it was going to say next. On the way to the park, it said, *She's wrong, and she's not fair: look at the way she said Rob was a hundred per cent normal tone-deaf success*. But at the pond – which she didn't even have to herself these days because lots of other kids had begun to dangle their feet in it after they'd seen her do it – it said, *She's right: if it were somebody else's mom who said that letting a kid go to the store was abuse or neglect or whatever, you'd think it was silly*. Of course, that wasn't what Mom had said, but you didn't need a little voice in your head to know what Aunt Joan had meant. Well, OK, but everybody knew Mom was afraid of . . . *Mom isn't afraid of anything (except Aunt Joan) for herself,* hissed the little voice. *It's you she's afraid for, and you know why.*

Nonsense! She yanked her feet out of the pond and put on her sandals. But the voice kept up. *You do, too, know why. You do. You do.*

She did. She did. And riding her bike home extra fast didn't help – it kept up so easily, not even the phantom Malachi could chase it away.

When she got home, she went straight to the piano and played the bell scale as loudly as she could. That drowned out the stupid voice – at least, it drowned it out enough so she could practise. But it was the wrong sort of day. The phone rang while she was still doing scales in the rhythms Aunt Joan had shown her, and when she was flexing her fingers before plunging into the arpeggios, Aunt Joan came bustling in, looking like Something Was Up. 'Sorry to interrupt, but I have a question for you.'

Uh-oh. 'Yes?'

'Would you be interested in taking piano lessons again next fall?'

'Well, um . . . I don't think Mom and Dad want me to. They're worried about—'

'I know they are. But when I told them how well you were doing, they said it would be all right for you to start again.'

Erin looked down at her hands, thinking of the way Con's fingers flashed over the keyboard. *You have to train them. And I bet that teacher of yours hasn't taught you how.* 'With the same teacher?'

Aunt Joan cleared her throat. 'Actually, part of what

I suggested was that you study with a real professional I know. Your mother agreed—'

'She did?'

'As soon as I told her he was a big name, she did,' said Aunt Joan crisply.

She's down on Mom again, whispered the little voice. *Careful.*

'Anyway, I called him. He just called back. And on the basis of what he heard in the background, he said he'd take you.'

In the background . . . 'You mean, he heard *me*? All I was doing was scales!'

'Erin, honey, you have no idea how impressive those scales sound – especially to someone who finds out you didn't know C major from E major three weeks ago. When I told him you had taught it all to yourself, with only an occasional assist from me on the fingering, he said he would take you.'

'I . . . um . . . that's . . . great.'

Aunt Joan patted her on the shoulder, which Aunt Joan didn't usually do. 'It sure could be. He's an old-world pianist, looks kind of like a lion, and acts like one, too, if his students aren't disciplined, which is a problem in these days of false praise and encouragement. But you are disciplined—'

'I am?'

'Well,' said Aunt Joan consideringly, 'maybe "obsessed" would be a better word for it, when it comes to the piano. Reminds me of— Never mind. In any case, it will do.' She glanced down with the famous Aunt-Joan-sees-right-into-your-mind look. 'There's one condition, though. You have to be able to read music.'

The little voice screamed, *WHAT!?* so loudly that for a second she thought she'd said it. But when she realized she hadn't, she managed to croak, 'I thought you said it was all right to learn music by ear.'

'It is. But it's not enough. A professional pianist needs an educated eye as well as a trained ear and athletic fingers. That's just the way it is. Don't worry. Mr Stesikowski – that's his name – isn't expecting fluency in five weeks. All he wants is knowledge of the two clefs, and ability to read basic chord patterns.' She rummaged around on the back of the piano, where all the music books were stacked up. 'So I said I'd teach you those. Let's start with clefs.'

Chord patterns. Two clefs. Fifth-grade reading. Erin felt her stomach move into a major earthquake, but Aunt Joan had already opened a spiral notebook and set it on the music rack.

'Let's look at it historically. Once upon a time, when people started writing notes down, they drew eleven lines, put middle C on the centre line, and the other notes on lines and spaces in each direction, like the keys on a piano. Those eleven lines covered all the notes human voices could sing. And this is what they looked like.'

Erin looked, blinked, and looked again.

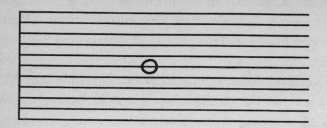

My gosh. How was she ever going to do this? It made her dizzy.

Aunt Joan smiled. 'Guess what – it was hard to read.'

Erin looked up at her. 'Even for normal people?'

'Of course. There were too many lines. And what's more, there was too much range to be useful. Look how many notes those eleven lines cover.' She reached two Fs down and two Gs up from middle C. 'Can you sing all that?'

'No way!'

'Nobody can. And there were – and still are – precious few instruments that have that kind of range. For example, if you play the flute, the lowest note you can play is middle C. So writing the other lines just took up a lot of paper in the days before there was paper – plus confusing the flautist. So one bright guy (I like to think he was the cousin of the guy who made up the blocks with letters on them, but he was several centuries earlier, so he probably wasn't) pointed out you could divide the thing up into five-line groups, which is what a staff is. You can choose your group from almost anywhere in the eleven lines, but you have to let people know which five you've chosen. That's why you put in a clef sign. For the piano, which has a huge range, you use the five lines on the top, the five lines on the bottom, and a short line for middle C.' She drew a note with a line through it between the two staffs. 'There. Isn't that easier?'

Not easier enough, but at least it explained why middle C had a line of its own. Maybe that was good; it was the only one she knew.

'And here's how we let people know what groups we chose. Put both your thumbs on middle C, and reach a fifth each way. What do you get?'

Erin played the fifths, silently thanking Con. Maybe she should try to get back to the window again. It wasn't his fault she'd shown up on a bad day. 'You get an F in the bass hand and a G in the treble.' A little bell went off in her mind. 'Oh.'

'Exactly,' said Aunt Joan. 'And that happens to be two lines up or two lines down on the staff. And each clef circles around the fifth.' She opened a music book and stuck it in front of the spiral notebook. 'See how they work?'

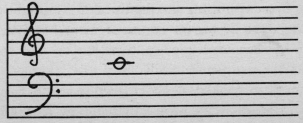

She did see – at least, she understood the principle. That was different from seeing what note was what, but working with Aunt Joan had taught her that if you hung onto the principle long enough, eventually what you saw began to make sense. It was just a matter of time. Five weeks. If only she lived in Sir Piers's world, none of this would be necessary.

'Erin? Do you get it?'

'Yes.' She sighed. 'I was just wishing I lived way back when, before they wrote down the eleven lines. Then I'd be normal.'

'DON'T SAY THAT!'

Omigosh, an Aunt Joanism! Right out of the blue. She looked at the friendly insides of the piano, wishing her own insides would stay put.

'Look,' said Aunt Joan, more softly, but no less scarily. 'Let's get some things straight. First of all, *normal* does not mean *right*. It means *the way people do things now*. Got that?'

She was going to be sick, right here on the floor. The world was starting round and round.

'Saying you wish you were normal is like being imprisoned in a castle tower and trying to escape by sitting in a corner and making up an imaginary world for yourself to live in. Tell me now – would that do any good, if you wanted to get out?'

'No,' she whispered dizzily.

Aunt Joan looked at her carefully, and her voice got a little less scary. 'You can see how it wouldn't do any good; can you see how it would do harm?'

'To the castle?'

'No, to you. Think. There you sit, day after day, living a perfect life in your imaginary world. One day, your fairy godmother – or your faithful minstrel, or your long-lost lover – tosses a rope in the tower window, so you can climb down a hundred feet and escape. What happens?'

Look at her face, look at her face, shouted the voice. *It's a trick question – you need a hint*. But Aunt Joan's face was too scary to look at for long. She'd just have to give the only answer she could think up. 'Um – I guess I try to tie a knot and . . .'

'Are you sure? Wouldn't it be more pleasant just to keep living in your imaginary world?'

'But then I'd never get out!'

'Exactly,' said Aunt Joan. She took a deep breath and looked out the window. When she finished, her face looked smaller and sadder. 'All right,' she said, sighing. 'I'll leave you alone. Just think about what you said.'

She didn't think about it then, but in the middle of the night it woke her up. She lay there, staring at the boxes of bottle caps in the yellow glow of the streetlight, thinking some more. Too bad thinking didn't do any good; she'd done more of it since she'd come here than she could remember doing in her life before, and all it had gotten her was . . .

She sat up, completely awake. A piano. And not just a piano – a piano playing Con's Mozart concerto. After putting a needle arm down on that passage four or five times, she'd know it anywhere. For a few minutes, she refused to let herself get up. If he was practising again, he was probably just as grouchy as he had been before, and she'd be wasting her time. But it was going right. It sounded really good, in fact. She tiptoed down the hall and carefully closed the little-room door behind her, expecting to see Con's music room develop out of the mist in the window.

But the big, dark object that gradually became clear wasn't a piano, and the light around it wasn't coming in through windows. The castle? How could it be? There were no pianos at the castle, and in Sir Piers's day Mozart hadn't been invented yet. She blinked a couple of times, expecting the scene to change or the piano to stop. Neither happened, so when everything settled down, she stepped out onto the ramparts.

The piano cut off in the middle of a phrase, as if somebody had pushed the off button on a CD player. In its place were shouts, neighs and the murmur of a crowd. She ran to the battlements and looked over.

It was like looking into fairyland. The early-morning sun glistened on the centre peaks of a city of brightly coloured silken tents that filled the plain from the moat to the distant woods. Between the tents, cobs quietly cropped the short grass, and chargers paced round and round on picket lines, their heads dropping low, then rocketing up, crests bent and ears pricked forward. Attendants in hundreds of different liveries watched them carefully, running forward to stop them when they began to paw chunks of turf into the air. Trotting back and forth between the tents, dogs like Malachi met, sniffed and circled back as the pages who were polishing armour and swords called them. In the middle of everything, decked with banners of all descriptions, stood the lists.

The tournament. She'd lucked out.

But not yet. There was no action out there, and from the sound of things, there was a lot of action in the courtyard. She crossed the parapet and looked down. It was as full as it had been the day of Giles's strategy, but this time, nobody was armed. Knights in glorious tunics stood everywhere, and this time, for a change, there were ladies, all dressed in low-cut, colourful gowns and wimpled headdresses. Squires and pages were everywhere, making detours as they ran errands so they could peek into the empty aisle that led to the raised, brightly carpeted platform in the middle of the courtyard. The murmur of talk rose to where she was; it sounded like the conversation of the audience just before Shakespeare in the Park plays, with everyone waiting for the actors.

Suddenly, six men in Sir Piers's colours stepped out of the arcade and raised straight, bannered trumpets to their lips in a fanfare that sent shivers down her spine. As they finished, the double doors behind them burst open, and a band of musicians playing viols, lutes, wooden flutes and drums marched slowly towards the central platform. Behind them walked Sir Piers, his blue tunic and mantle catching the first rays of sun that came over the ramparts. Twenty knights, some of them white haired and stiff, followed him, each stopping at an appointed place so they lined the sides of the aisles between the arcade and the platform. The musicians brought their march to a close; in silence, everybody strained forward to see. At a signal from Sir Piers, the six trumpeters played a new fanfare; on its concluding notes, ten squires dressed in white tunics started down the aisle between the ranks of knights. She could see Giles right away; he was half a head shorter than everyone else, but he walked like a prince.

The musicians started again, and to the haunting beat of drums, the squires walked to the platform and stood in a line facing Sir Piers. There was a sudden flurry as pages handed swords to the knights who lined one side of the aisle, and rowelled spurs to those on the other side. Then the knights paced up the platform steps and surrounded the white-clad squires. Behind them, pages carried hauberks, helmets and other pieces of armour.

When everyone was assembled, Sir Piers turned towards the stable and raised his hand again. Six different trumpeters stepped out from under that arcade, playing a signal to charge as they cleared a path through the crowd to the platform. Following them, ten grooms led ten fully caparisoned chargers with shields hanging from their saddles. The horses tossed their heads as they saw the crowd, their ornamented bridles glinting silver and their enormous feet thundering as they pranced.

It was right out of the wonderful Tennyson poem that Rob had read her. Too bad she had to watch from way up here instead of— Wait! *Did* she have to watch from up here? Why should she? Nobody could see her. She wouldn't get lost if she paid attention to where she was. If she went down, she could slip right through the crowd and be in the very front row when Giles was knighted.

She looked around the ramparts, trying to decide which was the best way down. The shortest route was to go down the stairs of any one of the towers on her treble side, but that would land her near the stables; she'd have to work her way through those excited horses, and they'd probably sense her, which would complicate things no end. It would be smarter to go down the stairs she usually took and edge along the wall until she was directly opposite the platform. She took a good, long look and started towards the tower door, feeling very brave.

The further she circled down the stairs, though, the louder the crowd noises grew. By the time she reached the door to Sir Piers's room, she'd more or less decided it would be a lot safer to watch through his windows. Ignoring the little voice that told her she was a chicken, she slowly lifted the latch – and staggered back against the wall as Malachi leaped though the opening.

'Malachi!' she whispered, as loudly she dared. 'Malachi!'

He didn't even give her a backward glance – just shot down the stairs in a scurry of toenails. Oh, no! What had she done? He was going straight towards Sir Piers, of course, and he'd mess up the whole ceremony. Her cheeks flaming bright scarlet, she raced down the stairs and got to the bottom just in time to see him worm his way through the crowd of kitchen boys who were packed into the doorway. There was nothing for it but to follow him. She chose the two smallest boys and pushed her way between them, praying that she was still invisible. Neither of them paid any attention, but when she looked back after she'd passed them, each one gave the other a shove. OK – now for Malachi. Fortunately, he cleared a little path for her, and gradually, edging her way between visiting pages, nudging ladies here and ducking under knights' elbows there, she began to catch up with him.

But the closer she got to the platform, the harder it was for both of them to move. She wormed her way forward, terrified that any second he'd find a hole and leap onto the platform. How close where they to the platform, anyway? Somewhere ahead of her, she could hear Sir Piers say, 'This sword has been used only to defend honour and justice. Take it, carry it, and be worthy of it,' but all she could see was Malachi's tail vanishing behind a knight's mantle. She could hear the jingle as the spurs were bound to the squire's feet, but all she could see was a man looking down in annoyance as the dog pushed past him. But they must be pretty close to the front now: people were so closely packed together that even Malachi couldn't get through. As he stopped, baffled, she dove forward and grabbed his collar. He gave a startled yelp, but she had him, and when he turned to look at her, he knew who she was.

'Sit!' she whispered fiercely. He obeyed, and when she looked up, panting in relief, she found out how long the chase had taken, and what a close call it had been. She was standing right below the platform in the front row. Five of the squires had been knighted, and they had taken their places on the side of the platform next to the horses, hauberks and helmets glistening, swords belted to their waists and spurs affixed to their heels. Near her were the others – and Giles was one of them. She stroked Malachi's head with the hand that wasn't holding his collar. He'd gotten her a front-row seat.

Sir Piers stepped towards the tallest remaining squire, holding a splendid sword by its richly carved scabbard. The squire stepped forward and kissed its hilt. As if that were a signal, two other knights bent down and strapped the spurs on his mail-shod feet, while Sir Piers intoned, 'Let these never be hacked off in shame or degradation.' Rising to their feet, the knights turned and took a heavy hauberk from the pages waiting behind and slid it over the squire's white tunic. As she watched, a small movement among the waiting squires caught Erin's eyes. It was nothing – just Giles, glancing at his watch . . .

His *what*?

She looked again, but of course she couldn't see anything; he'd dropped his arm to his side. But she'd been sure . . .

The two knights finished adjusting the hauberk and laced the helmet to it; smiling, Sir Piers stepped forward, his hands extended to belt the sword around the squire's waist, his voice intoning the words she'd heard as she'd edged through the crowd. After the sword was buckled, Sir Piers smiled at the squire and said, 'Bend your head; I am about to give you the *colée*.' The squire braced himself as Sir Piers raised his hand – and cuffed him on the side of the neck. Erin stared. It was obviously part of the ceremony, but in spite of his preparation, the new knight almost fell over, and when he regained his balance, he looked a little faded.

Come to think of it, everything looked a little faded. The blue of Sir Piers's cloak, the red and green of the two knights, the bright colour of the platform carpet – all the colours were disappearing the way they did after sunset. She looked around at the horses, the pages, the crowd – they seemed to be dissolving before her very eyes. Even Malachi's collar, clenched in her fingers, felt curiously insubstantial. In panic, she looked back at the platform. In the middle, superimposed on Sir Piers and the other knights, was her window, humming with expectancy. As she stared at it, disbelieving, something white flashed in front of her, and somebody stepped towards the frame. Giles. At the very edge of the window, he looked back, his face full of regret. Then he disappeared.

Behind her, everything went from grey to dark. There was nothing for it; if she didn't want to disappear with everything else, she had to follow him. Giving the fading Malachi a farewell pat, Erin scrambled up the misty steps to the vanishing platform and leapt through the window herself.

16
A Concerto Contest

The moment she jumped, she thought better of it. Where on earth she was going to end up? Was she going to end up on earth? It was taking an awfully long time . . . She landed with a thump, her heart beating fast, and looked around. Boy, Con's attic had never looked so good. The only thing she had to worry about now was the way Con was going to feel about having a Champion Sneaker-Upper drop in on him.

'Con?' she whispered. Then, as no one answered, a little louder: 'Con?'

She jumped as a door banged shut. Behind her? There was nothing but the slanting roof – and her window, leading to the little room. Beside her, then. But there were no doors anywhere around. Except, of course, for the one at the bottom of the stairs.

He must have just left – and in a hurry, too. The lamp behind his sofa was on. Well, she'd be a good ecologist and turn it off for him before she went through her own window, which was a lot more conspicuous than it usually was. It would feel good to do something normal like switching off a light in the middle of all this crazy stuff. She stood on the sofa's sagging cushions, reached over the back for the lamp – and gasped.

Spread out on a huge piece of green felt behind the sofa was a castle. *The* castle. There were the ramparts, just the way she'd seen them an hour ago. There were the towers, the portcullis, the courtyard, the arcades. Outside the castle, on a long green strip of felt between a blue paper moat and a forest of model trees, was the city of square tents, manned by a few pages, a pack of lead deerhounds and hundreds of chargers, fully armed. Between the tent city and the castle stood a stockade of popsicle sticks and a list made of pieces of moulding. But nobody was there. All the guards, pages and squires were inside the courtyard, grouped around a platform. And standing on the platform with all the knights who weren't permanently moulded into riding position, was Sir Piers.

She stared at it, her mind whirling. It wasn't real. It was just blocks – *the* blocks, from the toy chest. And the knights . . . at least, they looked like the knights. She got off the sofa and moved very carefully around to the back. Slowly she lifted the figures off the courtyard platform. Sir Piers. A knight in red. A knight in green. Pages in blue. Yes, they were the same, except not broken, of course. Well, that shouldn't be a surprise;

Aunt Joan had told her all the kids in the Family had played with them. But . . .

She pursed her lips, looking at them. Standing near Sir Piers and the other knights was a line of squires. They weren't dressed in white, of course, because their costumes were painted, but five of them were standing near fully caparisoned horses, and four others were waiting for action. Where was the fifth? Something bumped against her foot; looking down, she saw a squire in crimson, with dark bobbed hair and grey eyes. Giles, standing way apart from the tournament and even the castle, as if he'd just left. Which he had.

Giles. Con. Con. Giles.

Was that why she'd always gotten back here after she'd visited the castle? It had to be. That meant— No, she was crazy.

But was it any crazier to think you'd gotten into somebody's imaginary world than to think you'd gotten into the real life of a ghost?

She stood there, looking down. Somewhere in her mind, she could almost see Sir Piers stepping forward to hand the sword to the next squire, but when she listened for castley sounds, all she heard was cars crunching on the driveway below her and car doors slamming. She peered out the window – the real window, not hers – and saw ten or twelve antique cars, all different colours with fins. And getting out of them were parents and grown-up children, Rob's age, clutching yellow-bound music books. No wonder

Con had gone downstairs in such a hurry. This seemed to be the concerto contest. Maybe she could just slip downstairs and . . .

And everything was fading again, not to mention swirling. The light, the knights, the attic – when everything stopped, she was standing in almost total darkness, and the only sound was a piano. Dizzily, she dropped to her knees. On her way down, her hand touched something square and solid. She ran her fingers over it, and came to a metal handle. It felt like – it was! A toy box. She was back at Aunt Joan's, then. But the piano? As her eyes adjusted to the light, she looked behind her. The window was a perfect blank; the music couldn't possibly be coming from there.

She groped her way to the door. As she opened it, the piano got louder. Aunt Joan again? If it was, she was playing an awful lot faster and more fluently than you would think somebody whose fingers were as stiff and swollen as Aunt Joan's could play. But maybe she was just being unfair. During the daytime, Aunt Joan played for her, so she could learn new pieces; that meant playing relatively simple things. Maybe at night she played the stuff she really liked. Except that was no reason to be playing Con's concerto.

All right. This time, she wasn't going to let silly ideas about ghosts turn her into a chicken. Taking a deep breath, she walked down the hall, eased her way down the steps, carefully testing for bottle-cap boxes with her toes, tiptoed through the downstairs hall . . .

Trembling, she stopped at the door, peering into the part of the living room that didn't hold the piano. It wasn't completely dark; the streetlights lit it up. It looked so reassuringly shabby that she looked around the doorjamb.

And saw Uncle Druce.

Except it didn't look like Uncle Druce. It couldn't be anyone else – scruffy hair and beard, glasses, stooped shoulders – but the way he sat, the way his hands moved, the way he bent over the keys, the way he was totally absorbed in the sound . . . He looked like a whole different person from the shambling old man who collected bottle caps.

She slipped inside the door and sat on the rug, leaning against a bookcase full of catalogues, watching and listening. For a terrible moment, she was afraid he'd seen her, because he stopped. But he didn't turn round; he just sighed and started again. As he played, he looked out the window at the streetlight – then suddenly the streetlight wasn't there any more. Neither was Uncle Druce – at least, not completely. He seemed to be turning into a ghost; not the costume kind, but the real thing, transparent, only with an outline, so you could still see where he was. Behind him – maybe through him – the window began to flicker the way the window in the little room did, only more like an old TV warming up. And slowly appearing on its screen was the music room at Aunt Joan's house upstate, filled with people in good clothes, sitting uncomfortably in unfolded folding chairs. Con was one of them, most uncomfortable of all in a suit and bow tie, his cowlicks slowly rising out of his carefully greased hair. Not too far from him, directly opposite the two pianos, a man and a woman were sitting in real chairs, holding scores. They were wearing badges that said HAROLD PERKINS, JUDGE and SUSAN SIMPSON, JUDGE, so it was obviously the concerto contest. And taking her seat at the piano nearest the audience was a girl about Rob's age in a period dress and haircut. An older man – her teacher, probably – sat down at the other piano, and played what Con had explained was the orchestral part of her concerto. As he reached the place where the piano would join the orchestra, he looked up and nodded at the girl.

The second she came in, you could see why Con had been so nervous about this contest. She was truly awesome, and the longer she played the more awesome she got. The concerto really showed her off – lightning-fast runs, arpeggios all over the place, thundering octave scales – and she played them all with the kind of ease you saw with really good tennis players. A finger athlete – that's what she was, but it wasn't all she was. The phrasing was good, and the whole thing was one hundred per cent convincing. When she finished, the audience applauded enthusiastically, and the two judges looked at each other and nodded.

They didn't nod after the next two people, though.

Neither did anybody else, except maybe their parents, who were looking on anxiously. *Little Error plays so sweetly for Mommy and Daddy's guests*. It wasn't kind to sneer like that, of course, but as soon as they started, you knew exactly what Con meant. There wasn't anything wrong with the way they played; it was probably a mirror image of the notes on the page. But there wasn't anything right with it either. Lots of practice, but no imagination . . . No, she would not be mean. At least, not until she was absolutely sure she could do better.

When the second one finished, the audience fidgeted a bit in the uncomfortable chairs, and a couple of them even began to get up, but Mrs Simpson stopped them. 'One more: Druce Harding.' And Con stood up.

Erin stared at the window, feeling her jaw drop. Con – her sort-of friend, with his jokes, his imaginary world, his piano-playing – was *Uncle Druce*? She tried to focus on the ghostly figure at the real piano. All she could see was the outline . . . but that outline sat at the piano in exactly the same way Con sat on the bench in the window. And when Con's teacher had finished playing the opening bars of the Mozart concerto, Con lifted his hands with exactly the same gesture. It had to be the same person – Aunt Joan's little brother. *Oh, Con – what happened to you?*

Nothing had happened yet, that was for sure. Con's entrance was great – accurate, articulate and expressive

– and whatever his face might tell you, his hands weren't nervous at all. The people in folding chairs looked at each other; some of them nodded in appreciation, and Mr Perkins, who had been looking bored, sat forward. They were right to be appreciative; it sounded really good, really professional. It wasn't just that there were no mistakes – though she was relieved when he played the passage she had helped him with without improvising or adding extra measures. It wasn't just the good technique – probably, if you really knew your piano-playing, the older girl's was a bit better. It was the whole thing: the phrasing, the enthusiasm, the belief in the way it sounded. No wonder he spent so much time by himself in his attic with his silly jokes and his knights. The real Con was the Con that played the piano. How could you possibly share that with other kids?

For a minute, she wasn't sure whether she pitied him or envied him, but when he roared into the cadenza, there was no question in her mind. Envy. Clear, honey-dripping envy. To be able to play like that . . . heck, to be able to play half as well as that . . . she'd give up every kid she'd ever talked to at lunch, every sleepover she'd ever been to . . . everybody. Except Rob, of course. And she wouldn't miss one of them.

The cadenza came to an end, and Mr Roberts – was that his name? – finished up the last orchestra measures with a big smile on his face. As he played the concluding chords, the audience clapped with real enthusiasm, even the girl who had played so well. Con bowed – pretty gracefully, for Con – and sat down, looking tired. Judging from the number of grown-ups who nodded at him or leaned forward to pat him on the back, an awful lot of the Family had come to listen. But that was no big deal; the families of the other kids were there too, and they were all talking to each other and eyeing the judges, who were passing notes back and forth.

Finally, Mr Perkins stood up. 'We have a tie, here. That's not unusual, given the array of talent this contest generally draws. In the past, we have broken the tie by asking each of the leading contestants to improvise on a theme for two minutes, but last week, the sponsor of the contest decided that slanted the results in favour of those whose talents ran to jazz or composition rather than professional performance.'

Con's back stiffened.

'This year,' said the judge, 'the skill that will determine the winner is sight-reading. Each contestant will be given a piece of music he has not played before, and must play it to the best of his ability for two minutes.' He smiled at the audience. 'While everyone who has played this afternoon is excellent, two performances have been exceptional, and it is those two performers who will be sight-reading for us: Frances Walker and Druce Harding.'

In the scatter of applause that followed, Mr Roberts's hand shot up. 'Will the contestants have a few minutes to look over their music before they play it?'

The two judges glanced at each other; the woman shook her head. 'That would be unfair to whoever plays first, because the second person would have extra time to study the part.'

'Point taken,' said Mr Roberts. But he didn't look happy.

Neither did Con; he fidgeted in his chair, and his face looked even paler than usual. For just the second, superimposed on the audience, the pianos, and the judges, the shadowy image of the castle's lists appeared. Riding towards one end was a knight whose horse was caparisoned in crimson . . . but the whole scene faded as Mrs Simpson said, 'Druce and Frances, please come here and draw straws: the short straw goes first.'

Con got up, looking as if he were holding his breath; when Frances drew the short straw, his relieved sigh was audible. He sat down quickly in his chair, while Frances took the piece of music the judge handed her and set it on the music rack. She was nervous; you could see her hands shake as she lifted them to the keys. And no wonder! The piece was modern, and while there was a nice melody, the harmonies were dissonant, and the runs, when she came to them, were so chromatic that she stumbled all over the place. She was a pro, and she played for her full two minutes without stopping or going back, but when she got up, you could tell she *wanted* to cry, even though she was much too poised to do it in public.

'Very good,' said Mrs Simpson encouragingly. 'It's a difficult piece, and you did well with it. Druce?'

Con got up, took the music she handed him, set it on the piano rack – and plunged right in. Everybody sat forward, listening with a kind of awe. It was the same piece, but this time, the fanfare was stirring, accurate, vibrant. When he came to the runs, you knew he was playing them right; his hands flew over the keys, and above them, his face was a study in concentration. It was truly wonderful, and when he stopped, there was more applause than there had been for anything else, including the two best concertos. Con stood up and bowed, flushed with triumph. Erin hugged herself, smiling for all she was worth. He'd done it! He'd won! Everybody knew it – everybody, that is, but the judges, who were looking at each other in confusion.

'Just a minute, Druce,' said Mr Perkins as Con started back to his seat. 'Would you give us the music?'

The way he spoke made it clear that something was wrong. Silence settled over the room as Con took the music off the piano and handed to the judges. They looked at it, then at the other music in front of them, then at each other. Mrs Simpson cleared her throat. 'There has been a . . . a very strange mistake here. Both contestants played the same piece, but they were not given the same music.'

The audience stirred uncomfortably; across the

room, Mr Roberts threw Con an amazed look, then dropped his gaze to the floor.

'Druce,' said Mr Perkins, 'can you explain why you played the music Frances played instead of the music we gave you?'

Con's chin thrust itself forward. 'I thought it was the same.'

'How could you? She was given the third Bartók concerto; you were given the third Tchaikovsky.'

'The third Tchaikovsky!' Con rushed to the piano, dropped the music onto the bench beside him, and dove into the opening chords of the concerto he'd played on his stereo the first day she'd visited his attic. It sounded completely professional, but the judge stepped forward and stopped him.

'That's very effective,' he said, picking up the music, 'but you are clearly not sight-reading.'

'I'm playing it right, though! Look at the music, if that's what you believe in – I've got it note-perfect.'

The judge's puzzled look changed to one of annoyance. 'It's not a matter of what I believe in; it's a matter of what you can sight-read. Am I correct in assuming that the reason you could "sight-read" the Bartók was that you had studied it, too?'

'I haven't studied either of them,' said Con resentfully. 'I hadn't heard the Bartók since Dad was practising it, back when I was nine or ten; but when she played it, I remembered.'

A stir went around the audience; Frances looked at

Con with something close to envy.

'You have your father's ear,' said Mr Perkins, smiling slightly.

'It's not all ear,' said Con. 'He taught me how to use it. Once you know how to use your ear, you don't *need* to read notes. You can just listen.'

'And that's what you do? Just listen? Without consulting the page at all?'

'That's right.'

'Not even the words that should have told you you were dealing with Tchaikovsky, not Bartók?'

A ripple of laughter moved through the audience.

'Let's try again,' said Mr Perkins, smiling. 'As somebody who habitually ignores the page, you made a perfectly explicable error, for which I feel partly at fault. If we had explained that each person would play a different piece, you would have had to read at least the opening few chords. With your memory, however, it seems only fair to ask you to read something a little less obvious than a famous concerto.' He stepped back to the card table and picked up a third piece of music. 'Take a look at the cover this time, to give yourself a hint of what you're getting into.' He held it out.

Something about the way Con looked at it set off a faint buzzer in Erin's mind. *Take a look at it.* How many times had she heard teachers, tutors, psychologists say that to her? But not Con . . . it couldn't be . . .

The judge's eyebrows rose slightly. 'OK? You got it?'

'I think so,' said Con, his voice little more than a

whisper. 'Scriabin? I've heard of him, of course, but I don't really know any of his—'

'Excellent,' said the judge, opening the book on the music rack. 'Do what you can in two minutes. We're not expecting miracles – just a demonstration of essential competence.' He patted Con on the shoulder and went back to his chair. In his corner, Mr Roberts leaned forward anxiously as both judges looked down at their watches and nodded at Con to begin.

But Con didn't begin. He didn't even lift his hands to the keyboard. Erin squirmed as she watched. Anybody who had ever had stage fright could sympathize with that terrible frozen look . . . Then she heard her own voice in her head – *why don't you look at the music?* And he hadn't. Wouldn't. Well, he was looking at it now, and as she watched him, she suddenly knew exactly how: begging it to mean something, hoping desperately that if he kept staring at it, he would see what other people saw. A brightly dressed woman who was sitting with the Family leaned forward and whispered, 'Go ahead, honey.' Somehow, that only made the silence more terrible.

Finally, Mr Perkins looked up from his watch. 'OK, Druce,' he said kindly. 'Your two minutes are up. You may go back to your chair.'

Con got up as if he were a sleepwalker. For a moment, Erin wasn't even sure if he knew where his chair was, but he found it and sat down. Mr Perkins, who had been pretending to fiddle with his pencilled notes, stood up and said, 'We have heard an impressive array of talent this afternoon, in circumstances which are, like all performances, emotionally draining.' He glanced at Con's still, expressionless face and looked quickly away. 'It gives me great pleasure to announce the winner of the nineteen sixty-three Mohawk Valley Concerto Contest: Miss Frances Walker.'

Everybody applauded. Frances's parents hugged her, and as people began to get up, they clustered around her, congratulating her. But the congratulations were very subdued, and after looking at Con, who was frozen in his chair, staring out the window, everybody began to slip away, politely making excuses to the brightly dressed woman, who was trying to offer coffee and cookies as if nothing were wrong. Within a few minutes, there was nobody left but the Family and Mr Roberts.

As soon as she had closed the door behind the last guests, the brightly dressed woman – she had to be Con's mom – hurried back into the music room, wiping her eyes with a frilly handkerchief. 'Next time you finish second in a contest, Con, I hope you'll be more gracious about it. You didn't even shake that girl's hand, and the way you've been sulking here has driven everybody home. Your father would be ashamed of you.'

Con didn't look at her, but he mumbled something apologetic.

'You've got nothing to be sorry for,' said one of the

uncles heartily. 'You played fine, until that damn judge pushed you too hard. Losing's part of the game; you gotta learn how to do it.' He patted Con's unmoving shoulder. 'For this year, honourable mention is plenty good enough, and next year you'll take the cake.'

'I'm afraid it's not a question of honourable mention,' said Mr Roberts quietly. 'The judges told me that they're bound by the rules, and Druce didn't fulfil the conditions of the contest.'

'What!' said Con's mom. 'All that beautiful playing, and he doesn't even get his name in the paper?'

Mr Roberts sighed. 'I'm afraid that's the case. And I'm very, very sorry this has happened. If I had known about the change in rules, I would have insisted that Druce withdraw.'

'Withdraw!' said another uncle. 'Why would you have done that? The boy's a genius – it's just a question of experience!'

'It's very puzzling,' said Con's mom. 'I've never seen him freeze before.' She bent solicitously over Con. 'What went wrong, honey? Why didn't you play?'

Con looked away. 'Because I didn't know what to play.'

'But, honey! The notes were right in front of you.'

'So what?'

'What on earth are you trying to say?'

Con looked dully at Mr Roberts. 'I didn't know you knew.'

'I knew to some extent,' said Mr Roberts. 'That's

211

why I kept insisting that you pay more attention to the page. But since you always made your resistance a matter of principle, I . . .' He looked apologetically first at Con, then at the Family. 'I was remiss. I could easily have tested him, but because his insistence on the importance of ear-training seemed to be connected to his feelings for his father in such a fragile way, I was reluctant to push the issue. I only recently began to suspect there was a perceptual problem.'

'A perceptual problem!' said an aunt, joining the circle around Con. 'What do you mean?'

'He means,' said Con in a strange, dead voice, 'that I can't read notes. That's why I didn't play.'

'Oh no, dear,' his mom broke in hurriedly. 'You don't mean that. You're just discouraged. The little problem you had at first is—'

'Little problem!' said the first uncle. 'Edith – what is this?'

'It's nothing, I tell you!' she said, starting to cry. 'He's always had slight visual difficulties. That's why Jack trained his ear so well. But I always thought it was just compensation. I never *dreamed* he couldn't read notes.'

One of the aunts – maybe Aunt Agatha, though it was hard to tell with everybody looking so young – stooped down in front of Con. 'You can't read music at *all*?'

'I can kind of figure it out,' he said sulkily, 'but it takes me forever.'

'What about words? Are they a problem, too?'

'Of course not!' said his mom. 'He just doesn't like school, and of course, he practises so much . . . I mean, lots of talented kids repeat grades because of their outside interests!'

'Repeat grades!' Everybody gasped at once.

Erin looked desperately around the ring of half-familiar faces. Where was Aunt Joan? She was the only one who could stop them – not to mention the person who would know what to do. But there was nobody who looked even remotely like Aunt Joan.

And instead of the angry things she would say, there was just a babble of voices, some of them asking Con questions and others talking over his head. In the middle of everything, Con stood up.

'If you'll excuse me,' he said with exaggerated politeness, 'I'd like to go upstairs.' He began to thread his way between the empty folding chairs.

There was a buzz of surprised remarks, but Erin couldn't hear what they said, because the sound of Uncle Druce's piano-playing got louder, and Uncle Druce's silhouette got clearer. Behind him, she saw Con walk up the front stairs, along the hall, and up to his attic, his chin high and his shoulders tight. For a moment he just stood at the top of the stairs, growing clearer as Uncle Druce's angry improvisations softened and his silhouette faded again. Then his shoulders sagged, and he started slowly across the attic, undoing his bow tie and his top button. When he reached the sofa, he dropped the tie on it, then his coat. Stretching his arms idly, he stepped towards the side of the sofa.

Erin could hardly keep herself from jumping up. *Look out! Look out! You left Giles right by—*

Crunch.

Con lifted his foot quickly, looking down in surprise. When he realized what he'd done, he knelt down and picked up the little red figure – or what was left of it. For a second, he stared at it, his face a mixture of regret and disbelief. But gradually, his whole expression changed. Putting down the fragments of Giles on the sofa arm, he crawled forward to the city of tents. Slowly, he reached out, picked up one of the knights, and snapped off his head. Then he picked up a horse. Erin closed her eyes, but even through Uncle Druce's music, she could hear the snap of the legs. *Stop! Stop!*

But he didn't stop. Deliberately, expressionlessly, he picked up one lead figure after another, snapped it apart, laid it down, and went on to the next. The pages, dogs and chargers in the tent city. The guards and bowmen on the ramparts. The crowd of figures in the courtyard. When he came to the platform, she was sure he'd realize what he was doing, but he didn't. Snap, snap, snap. The green knight. The red knight. The squires. The horses. Finally he picked up Sir Piers with his right hand, moved his left hand up to finish the job – and hesitated.

Everything went quiet. There was no music now, and she could hardly see Uncle Druce's silhouette at all. Then, slowly, Con put Sir Piers down and looked around at the heap of broken figures. There was the sound of a sob – just one. Then he turned to the side, dragged one of the toy boxes from under the eaves, and pulled out some crumpled pieces of newspaper. The window began to fade, but before the streetlight fully reappeared, she could see Con sorting through the wreckage, dividing the knights into groups, then arranging them carefully and lovingly in layers to be put into the box. Then the window became just a window. And in front of it, a shadow against the streetlight, sat Uncle Druce, his face in his hands.

She got up, trying not to cry. Even when he'd been Con, he hadn't been the sort of person you could give a hug to. Now . . . She turned away, planning to tiptoe across the hall and up the stairs. But in the hall, with one finger to her lips, stood Aunt Joan.

17
Aunt Joan's Room

Aunt Joan climbed slowly up the stairs, the shuffle of her slippers barely audible in the silent house. Erin turned towards her room when they got to the top, but Aunt Joan touched her shoulder and opened the door to her own room, letting a little square of light into the hall. That seemed odd — you sort of got the feeling nobody went into Aunt Joan's room but Aunt Joan — but Erin followed her.

It was like stepping into another world. For one thing, while the other upstairs rooms were small, it was as big as the living room and dining room together. For another, though everything in it was old and nothing was tidy, it wasn't shabby at all. Instead of the thread-bare carpets and scuffed floors in the rest of the house, there were two beautiful big oriental rugs, and the floor was a warm wood brown. The bed was a four-poster with a canopy, and while of course it wasn't made in the middle of the night, you could see that the bedspread had beautiful patterns woven into it. Bookcases as tall as Aunt Joan lined two whole walls; they were filled with books, not bottle caps, and the long mantel their top shelf made was decorated with interesting statues and nicely framed old-fashioned photographs. In the corner where the bookcases ended, an antique desk loomed over a leather easy chair. Near them, in the bay window that overlooked the street, there was a bench of wonderful house plants in handsome pots. Erin closed the door behind her and stood transfixed.

Aunt Joan, who had been on her way to the desk, looked back with amusement. 'I forgot you hadn't seen my bower,' she said dryly. 'Just think – the whole house used to look like this, years ago.'

'What . . . what happened to it?'

'What happens to us all,' said Aunt Joan. 'It got older. I fought it a while – inside and out – after Jan died, but arthritis made the battle increasingly difficult. Then Druce moved in, and since he didn't care about how things looked, I confined my efforts to my own room.'

Erin thought of the day she'd seen Aunt Joan trying to pull weeds. 'Oh! Is that why the garden at your school is so much prettier—' She stopped, blushing as she realized how tactless that was.

Aunt Joan's eyebrows shot up. 'You've seen the school?'

'Yeah. When I was buying bread and milk last week, somebody told me where it was, and I rode down to look. I was going to tell you, but then Mom called and—'

'—And when you came home, you accidentally caught me in my least charitable mode.' Aunt Joan sighed. 'For which I am heartily sorry. My uncharitable mode is seldom fair, and you weren't meant to hear it. What did you think of the school?'

'I . . . I liked the waterfall. And the gardens. I couldn't see much beyond that, but the man in the store told me it was famous. I didn't know that.'

'No,' said Aunt Joan. 'I don't suppose you did. There was something of an argument in the Family when I married Jan; communications practically ended until he died.'

Her voice was sad, not uncharitable; maybe, just this once, it would be OK to ask questions about the Family. But as Erin opened her mouth, Aunt Joan held up a finger. 'Wait.'

Slowly, footsteps shuffled up the stairs, paused, and went on. A moment later, Uncle Druce's bedroom door clicked shut.

Aunt Joan sat down in the desk chair. 'Thank you,' she said. 'I'd just as soon he didn't know we heard him playing the piano. For that matter, I'd just as soon nobody else heard about it, either.'

'OK,' said Erin. But she couldn't help adding, 'Why?'

'Because . . .' Aunt Joan steepled her fingers and looked absently across the room. 'Because he's the Con you asked me about in the car that day. It gave me a real turn to hear you say his name, because nobody's used it for ages. It was the nickname I gave him when he was about two, because he kept on going to the piano and saying, "I con play it!" ' She sighed. 'And as he grew up, he played more and more beautifully. But he hasn't touched a keyboard for almost forty years.'

'Forty years! Then he never played after—' she changed direction just in time – 'after he was a kid?'

'That's right,' said Aunt Joan. 'I don't know exactly what happened – his mother said something about his losing a concerto contest, but that wouldn't have done it if there hadn't been trouble brewing for some time. And there had been. He was your age when our father died, which is tough on any kid. But in this case – well, take a look at that picture, and maybe you'll see.'

Erin looked at the picture she'd pointed to: sitting in front of a grand piano with an open lid, his arm along the top, was . . . 'Is that Uncle Druce?' The moment she'd said it, she realized it couldn't be. Not just because there was no beard; the eyes were too steady, the face too confident. 'No . . .'

'You did see,' said Aunt Joan. 'That's our father, at the age Druce is now – which was how old he was when Druce was born. They were thick as thieves, and not just about the piano. Everything – the knights, the castle— What's that you said, dear?'

'Um . . . nothing. It's just . . . sad he died.'

'It was more than sad, because Druce turned out to

be dyslexic as well as a talented pianist. Imagine what that did to a boy who'd spent the first six years of his life being billed as a prodigy! Dad was the one person with the clout to make him deal with it; my stepmother denied the problem entirely, and the rest of the Family was sold on the idea of his genius. So after Dad died, the poor kid had no effective support in facing his problems; not surprisingly, instead of working things through for himself, he retreated into a fantasy world that allowed him to think he could be a prodigy just the way he was. When reality punctured that, he was left with nothing.' She sighed. 'By the time Jan and I got back from a two-year stay in Europe, my gifted brother Con had turned into *Druce Harding who used to play the piano*. Such a waste.'

Erin thought of the way she'd looked around the room in the window downstairs for Aunt Joan when everybody was talking to Con at once. 'It's too bad you weren't there when he failed the contest or . . . whatever. It would have made a big difference.'

Aunt Joan glanced at her in something close to surprise, but the look faded into one of regret. 'That's very sweet of you, dear, but I doubt I would have been allowed anywhere near the scene. With the exception of Dad, the Family never got used to the fact that I married a Polish immigrant – even though this particular Polish immigrant happened to be the leading light in Eastern European educational thinking.'

'But your school! It could have *helped* Con!'

Aunt Joan shook her head. 'The school didn't exist yet. In fact, the school came into existence *because* of Con. Jan and I had talked about starting one, and the time was certainly ripe, because Jan's influence had finally brought learning disabilities to the attention of the American educational world. But Jan was a scholar; I don't think he would ever have taken on the administrative responsibilities of a school if I hadn't been so heartbroken about my little brother.' She smiled sadly. 'Bless him, he said if I couldn't save Con, we could at least save lots of others. So that's what we did.'

Somewhere in Erin's mind appeared the friendly face of the hardware store man, talking about his son. All those kids, saved because of Con. How strange. But how cool. 'And Con . . . I mean, Druce?'

'He dropped out of high school the day he turned sixteen and left home a week later. That was it, as far as the Family was concerned. The only gesture they made was to allow his mother to sell one of the pianos – the concert grand Steinway, which by Dad's will was supposed to be Con's – and give him the money, so he wouldn't disgrace them by pumping gas, washing dishes, or driving a truck.' Aunt Joan sighed. 'It seems not to have occurred to anybody that a boy with no direction, no morale and a lot of cash might invest it in something other than the stock market.'

Erin's eyes opened wide. 'You mean . . . ?'

'Of course I do,' said Aunt Joan. 'We're talking about

the sixties and seventies, and he lived in an underworld of drifters. I don't know the details – Jan and I were the only people in the Family with whom he kept up even tenuous connections, but we hardly saw him until he drifted into collecting bottle caps sometime in his mid-thirties. That's when he finally allowed Jan to teach him. It started, of course, with his need to read catalogues, but it became something intellectually rewarding.' She pointed to another of the photographs. 'He liked Jan a lot – for years he came over every Wednesday evening, and the two of them talked far into the night.'

Erin looked at the picture. It had been taken in the living room – she could recognize the easy chairs and the bay window behind them. But like Aunt Joan had said, nothing was shabby. In one chair, with his feet on the coffee table, was an old man with a tremendous shock of grey hair and an intelligent expression that made his face a lot different from the all-American faces in the Family. Seated on the other chair, leaning forward in a way that made you think the camera had caught him in the middle of a sentence, was a younger Uncle Druce, but the alert, sardonic expression on his face was Con's.

'Jan died two or three weeks after that was taken,' said Aunt Joan, looking at it sadly. 'The Family expressed its sympathy by welcoming me back to its bosom, for which Druce has never forgiven it – he was almost as torn up about losing Jan as I was.'

Erin studied the interesting face. 'I can see why Uncle Druce liked him.'

'Oh yes. He was a wonderful man – and the only close friend Druce had after Dad died, I think. That's one reason why I asked Druce to come live here; I hoped I could continue the kind of intellectual stimulation that was bringing him out of himself. But I overestimated myself: between grieving and the problems the school was having during the recession in the eighties, I had very little to offer anybody. By the time I emerged, so to speak, I was in constant pain with arthritis and Druce had completely sunk into those damned caps. I never quite lost hope, though; that's why I agreed to take the second piano after his mother died this spring. I thought maybe if it were sitting there, he might tinker with it. But I don't think he would have if you hadn't come.'

'If *I* hadn't come!?'

'Sure,' said Aunt Joan. 'You get absorbed in the piano just the way he used to – once you get started, the whole world disappears. Sometimes, when he's standing out in the hall, or sitting on the stairs, listening to you practise, I think back to the days I used to visit home – I'm twenty years older than Druce, so I wasn't around much when he was growing up – and watch our father listening to him. If it brought that back to me, imagine what it must have brought back to him.'

There was no way you could say you knew exactly what it brought back. But things were beginning to make a crazy kind of sense. 'I . . . I never knew he was listening.'

'No; he took care that you shouldn't. And that's why it's so important for us not to say a thing about the way he played tonight. If he's going to find his way back, he has to do it by himself.'

She could see that. Bouncing into breakfast with '*Hi, Uncle Druce! Heard you playing last night!*' just wouldn't make it. But understanding didn't make what Aunt Joan had said any less scary, if you lived in a Family that ditched the losers. Probably if it hadn't been so late at night and she hadn't been so tired and sorry for Uncle Druce, Aunt Joan and Jan, she would have just kept her mouth shut, but as it was, she heard herself say, 'Do you think there's any hope of my getting into sixth grade?'

'That depends as much on your school as it depends on you,' said Aunt Joan. 'If your school will accept a demonstration of real progress in place of fifth-grade reading skills, you'll probably be let in sixth on the condition that you work with a tutor. Anticipating that, I've called one of Jan's brightest students, who works in New York now, and he has said he'll gladly take you on.'

That shouldn't be disappointing, but somehow it was. 'So you don't think I could get to fifth-grade reading skills fast enough?'

'I can't promise you that,' said Aunt Joan, 'but I can promise you that in the long run, it won't make one iota of difference. In a year, if you keep working, you will be reading that Tennyson poem, as well as poring over the pictures. If you thought of it that way instead of worrying about grade levels, your black angel might back off, which would be all to the good.'

'My black angel? What's that?'

'It's the invisible figure that stands on your shoulder and whispers into your ear: *You can't do this. No matter how hard you try, you'll be stuck in fifth grade for the rest of your life. You're a disgrace to your parents. Everyone is ashamed of you. Nothing you do to help yourself will make any difference.*'

Erin stared at her. 'How did you . . . ?'

Aunt Joan smiled. 'In my business, honey, black angels come in hosts. They're extremely effective, too; most people aren't even aware of their presence, so they give into them without realizing they're doing it. But that's fatal. Once you've let your black angel determine your worth, you disappear.'

Disappear. Into a window seat. Into an attic. Into a castle in a window.

Aunt Joan looked across the room. 'In all the years I've been teaching, I've only seen one kid with a bigger black angel than yours. He just played the piano for the first time in thirty-eight years.'

That wasn't exactly true. It had to have been Uncle Druce who had been playing for the last couple of nights. But it wouldn't be polite to correct Aunt Joan, especially since . . . No, she couldn't be. People like Aunt Joan didn't . . . Well, maybe she was . . .

'Don't mind me,' said Aunt Joan, pulling a Kleenex out the box on her desk. 'And don't worry. Nobody is going to be ashamed of you, whether you're in sixth grade or fifth in the fall. Next time the Family hears about you, they're going to learn that you've inherited the musical gene. You'll be the latest sensation.'

'I . . . I'm not sure I want to be—'

'—A pianist?' Aunt Joan looked at her sharply.

'Uh-uh. The latest Family sensation.'

'Accept it,' said Aunt Joan gently. 'It's meant to be supportive, and so long as you recognize it for what it is, you'll be all right.'

That was a very strange thing for Aunt Joan to say. 'For what it is?'

'Maybe I should say, for what it isn't,' said Aunt Joan. 'In some families, love expresses itself in understanding, tolerance and forgiveness. In ours, unfortunately, it doesn't – but that doesn't mean it's not there, or that you can't return it. Just that it's extremely complex.'

Complex . . . confusing, was more like it. In the middle of all that, could anything be clear? Even . . . 'Do you *really* think I could be a pianist?'

'Oh, yes. If you work with Stesikowski, you'll be a very fine pianist in a comparatively short time. No miracles, mind you. We're talking about a lot of practice, and you'll have to learn to read music – at least well enough to use it as a map. But you can do it if you want to.'

As if being an awesome pianist was something you could possibly *not* want to be! It just seemed a little unbelievable, after all those days in school, staring at the page . . . she looked across the room at the beautiful house plants, thinking sleepily how wonderful it would be to play the piano like Con or Frances Walker.

Aunt Joan braced her hands on the chair arms and pushed herself to her feet. 'You know, it's three in the morning, and instead of talking about all these deep issues, we should go to bed.'

That seemed to be a dismissal; Erin started towards the door. But as she stepped out between the boxes of bottle caps into the shabby hall, she stopped and looked back at Aunt Joan, who was straightening an ornament next to the picture of Jan and Uncle Druce. 'Um . . . Aunt Joan?' She really hadn't known what she wanted to say, but when she saw how painful it was for Aunt Joan to lower her arm, she got an idea. 'You know, I really like flowers. So if you wanted somebody to help you weed the garden . . . I . . . well, I'd be glad to do it.'

There was a long pause; then Aunt Joan turned round. 'That's very kind of you,' she said huskily. 'Maybe I'll take you up on it.'

18
Solder

If you'd just walked in for breakfast the next morning, you would never have known that anything out of the way had happened the night before. Uncle Druce looked at a catalogue while he ate two pieces of toast with peanut butter; Aunt Joan looked at the newspaper while she ate one piece with grape jelly, and nobody said anything. But neither of them was reading, and the dining room felt as if everybody were being very careful with everybody else. Erin chewed as quietly as she could, hoping they hadn't noticed she'd noticed.

Apparently, they hadn't. At exactly 8:25, Uncle Druce stood up, put on his green jacket with JOE'S PARKING GARAGE on the back, and left for work. Aunt Joan poured herself a second cup of coffee, and when she'd finished it, she pulled out the reader and opened it to the chapter they'd started yesterday on two-syllable words.

'Now,' said Aunt Joan, 'I want you to read what's in front of you here—'

Erin felt her stomach churn as she looked at the blur of words. Read all that! She couldn't possibly have worked with all those words yesterday!

'—and every time your black angel starts yammering at you, I want you to say, *Shut up*.'

Oh. Erin swallowed hard. 'Once upon a time, there lived a little girl called . . .' Her fingers gripped the page. A name. It had to be a name, but she couldn't—

'*Shut up*,' said Aunt Joan. 'Come on, say it.'

'That wasn't a black angel! I couldn't figure out—'

'And who told you you couldn't figure it out?'

Erin looked up, puzzled. She knew the little voice that said terrible things when she was on bike rides was a black angel, but this – 'I thought it was me.'

'That's what it wants. You're playing into its hands. Tell it to shut up.'

'*Shut up*,' she said, not very convincingly. But as she looked at that terrible name again, she realized she knew the first word just fine: *Red*. And the one after the word she didn't know was *Hood* . . . 'Oh! Red Riding Hood!'

'Very good,' said Aunt Joan. 'Go on.'

'She lived in a . . . *Shut up*.'

'Active, isn't it? Look at that word. There's a word you know at the beginning of it – block it off with your finger.'

'*Cot* . . . Oh! *Cottage!*' She looked up again. 'But I

didn't read it! I put it together!'

'It's aggressive, too. Every time you do something intelligent, like putting a word together — which is, incidentally, what everyone does when they read — it undercuts you. Go on.'

'. . . she lived in a cottage at the edge of a— *Shut up.*'

Aunt Joan stood up. 'You've got the idea. While I do the dishes, see how far you can get. Underline the words you can't figure out — but not until you've blocked off words inside them that you can read. You know the first three letters of that word, for instance.'

'*For* . . . Oh. *Forest*! How dumb of—'

'*Shut up,*' said Aunt Joan, collecting the plates.

They were putting the sandwiches on the table when Uncle Druce got home, because he was late, and Aunt Joan had a board meeting for the school at 1:15.

'Sorry,' he muttered, putting down the bag he was carrying. 'Had to stop by the hardware store.' As Aunt Joan went out to the kitchen for the tea, he looked at Erin. 'I guess Mike really took a shine to you.'

'Mike?'

'Guy who runs the hardware store.' For the first time since she'd come, Uncle Druce smiled. 'Gave me a soldering iron, just like that, and sent you his regards.'

'Oh! I'd been meaning to tell you he said—'

Uncle Druce put his finger on his lips as Aunt Joan came back in, and Erin looked down quickly at her plate. When she looked up again, Uncle Druce was leafing through a catalogue. He never once looked up all through lunch, but the way Aunt Joan glanced at him from time to time suggested she knew he wasn't really reading.

She'd halfway expected him to say more after Aunt Joan left, but he went upstairs, so she did the dishes. Maybe she'd do a little weeding, to surprise Aunt Joan when she got home. She yawned as she reached for the dishtowel. But first, she'd take a—

Something thumped against the woodwork behind her. Turning round, she saw Uncle Druce ease the toy box through the door. 'If you want to fix those knights,' he said, 'we better get going. Can you fetch the soldering iron while I get this down to the basement?'

She zipped into the dining room while he struggled with the basement door, then followed him down the stairs, through a junkyard of broken furniture, past the washer and the dryer, around the furnace – and into a room with dirty little windows that looked out onto the bushes around the base of the house. As he put down the toy box and switched on the light, she saw it was a workshop – and surprisingly neat, considering. There were boxes of bottle caps and scrap lumber in all the corners, but there was no clutter on the workbench, and the tools were hanging up neatly just above it.

'This is going to take some time,' he said, taking the

soldering iron from her. 'But at least we don't have to sort them. Let's take them out layer by layer and line the layers up along the wall, so we can see what we've got.'

She nodded and opened the lid, wondering when he'd checked the layers. It had only taken her two or three minutes to do those dishes. But of course, he'd had plenty of time when she was practising the piano, and he was listening. As the two of them lifted out the knights layer by layer, she felt the air hum with all the things she couldn't say. Sir Piers, Malachi, the one whole knight and the pages. A broken knight in red; a broken knight in green; ten broken knights in full armour, twelve broken horses, a smashed squire in crimson. Bowmen, guards, lancers, horses, all broken. Looking over the parapet, she'd seen every one of them − whole, alive, moving − but there was no way she could tell him.

If they brought back memories to him, though, you'd never have known it. He slid the new soldering iron out of its box, muttering as he struggled with the staples that held it in place. When he had plugged it in to heat up, he opened the little box of what looked like wire, cut off a piece, and held the end of it to the tip of the iron with a pair of pliers. A little blob of molten metal dropped onto the workbench. 'All set,' he said. 'You match heads to bodies and put them here on the bench; I solder. OK?'

'OK,' she said dubiously. 'But I'm not sure I can . . .'

Shut up, said Aunt Joan's voice in her head. 'Um, that is . . . sure.'

She could do it, too, but like he said, it took a long time. Every time she was just about ready to say, *Agh, that's close enough*, she thought of the castle in the window, and the real imaginary people who had lived in it; obviously it would make a difference to them. She was so busy trying to do them justice that she didn't even think about Uncle Druce until she scooped up the pieces of the smashed squire in crimson and put them on the workbench.

He reached for it automatically, but as his hand closed on all the pieces, he looked down, then shook his head. 'Not this one. I'm afraid it's too far gone.'

But it's Giles! You can't just . . . ! 'Um, you can't do anything for it at all?'

He organized the fragments until they were more or less where they'd have to go. 'Well, I can sort of stick him together, I suppose, but I don't see much point. He'll never be what he was.'

'But he'll be more than just pieces!'

Uncle Druce shrugged. 'OK.' He went to work on it, and she went on to the next layer of knights, carefully not watching. But all that tact was wasted; all afternoon he stayed in his bubble. Sometimes, when he stretched his fingers, he looked sort of thoughtful as he glanced at the knights who were finished, but all she had to do was take the kind of breath you take before you're going to talk, and he quickly turned back to his soldering. The silence got louder and louder, until he finally straightened up, stretched his shoulders, and said, 'That's it for today.'

'OK,' she said, trying to keep the disappointment out of her voice.

He looked at the fixed knights; it wasn't until now that she realized he'd arranged them in matching groups. 'Well,' he said, 'you can sure tell they've been mended.'

'Sure. But they all stand up OK.' She frowned at the silver joints. 'Do you have some paint?'

'Not the right kind. I'll ask Mike tomorrow.'

She sighed, quickly changing it to a cough in case he should think she was ungrateful. 'Should we wrap them up?'

'Leave them out. Won't do them any harm, and it takes solder a while to cool.'

'OK,' she said. And added, 'Thank you very much.'

If he heard her, there was no sign of it. He picked two medium-sized nails out of the jars that lined the wall under the dirty windows, drove them into the plywood over the bench, and stuck the soldering iron between them. And that was that . . . Except when she looked at the knights on the bench, they seemed very forlorn. They didn't belong down here. They belonged . . . That was it! They belonged to Sir Piers, and he was still lying on a piece of newspaper. She scurried across the room and picked him up – Malachi too, for good measure – and put him with the others.

Much better, but that wasn't fair to William and the other whole pages, so she went to fetch them too. When she turned round, Uncle Druce had picked up Sir Piers and was looking at him thoughtfully, but as she stopped, trying to think of the right thing to say, the back door banged upstairs.

'Joan's back,' he said, putting Sir Piers down carefully. 'Let's go up and see what's for dinner.'

What was for dinner was canned beef stew and baked potatoes – definitely not memorable, but in this house you only ate to survive anyway. The only suggestion that something unusual had happened was that after dishes, Uncle Druce went down to the basement. Erin started to follow him, but he shook his head. That's when she realized why he had chosen an afternoon Aunt Joan was gone to fix the knights. Of course! He knew that she didn't know they were broken, and he wanted to keep it that way.

She wandered in to the piano, wondering what he was doing. She wanted to think he was looking at the knights and remembering. But he was probably checking the solder and tidying up the bench. Sighing, she sat down and played Bach's hymn to piano-tuning. It sounded good, but somehow she wasn't in the mood for that sort of thing, and she was too sleepy to do really industrious scale-practising, so she started to diddle. 'Three Blind Mice', with chords in the bass. It wasn't very interesting, but as Con said, it was a beginning. Maybe she should try it as a waltz. She fiddled around with the chords in the bass . . . *ump-chuck-chuck, ump-chuck-chuck* – there. Then she added the mice in the treble. Hey, not bad! She could do it!

She couldn't do it splendidly, though. It needed octave runs and trills and all sorts of fancy things she couldn't manage yet. If only Uncle Druce would come out of his bubble, he could show her so much! Well, Mr Stesikowski would teach her technique, and then she'd be able to improvise really well. In the meantime, back to 'Frère Jacques' in fourths with bells in the bass, which was beginning to sound impressive. She played the opening bars . . . not quite impressive enough. Funny, it had sounded all right yesterday. Maybe her standards were getting higher. Or maybe it was the creepy feeling that she wasn't playing only for Con, who was usually her audience these days. It really felt as if somebody were watching her. Still playing, she glanced into the dining room, but Aunt Joan was working the crossword puzzle. Nope, just imagination working overtime again; back to work. *Dormez vous, dormez vous* . . . No, darn it, she could *feel* somebody . . . she glanced over her shoulder, and stopped.

Uncle Druce was standing three feet behind her.

'Shove over,' he said, gesturing towards the bench.

Unbelievable. Awesome. Fantastic. 'Which way?' she said. 'Bass or treble?'

'You play bass,' he said. 'Those bells sound pretty

good, but you can't play an octave run worth a darn.'

She scooted over. In the dining room, Aunt Joan looked up from the crossword puzzle.

'All right,' said Uncle Druce, sitting down. 'Same piece. You start. And don't stop, you hear? Keep going, even after I come in.'

ALL THE KING'S HORSES
Laura C. Stevenson

It began the day Grandpa escaped . . .

Something very odd has happened to Colin and Sarah's much-loved grandfather. It's as if a stranger is inhabiting his body . . . as if Grandpa has been spirited away and a changeling left in his place. Raised all their lives on his tales of great heroes and fantastical legendary creatures, Colin and Sarah feel sure that the Faer Folk are involved.

In an attempt to find him again, they follow Grandpa's path, crossing the boundary between the everyday world and the enchantments of the Otherworld . . .

A wonderfully lyrical fantasy adventure brimming with characters from the Otherworld – from magnificent horses to mischievous night-elves and the legendary Sidhe.

'Full of power, excitement, pertinent observation, humour and sheer *readability*'   *Carousel*

ISBN 0 552 547182

ABOUT THE AUTHOR

Laura Stevenson grew up in Ann Arbor, Michigan, the University town in which she was born, but 'home' to her was the Vermont farm that became her parents' summer place when she was five years old. During her Vermont summers, Laura began the day by practising the violin for three hours in the loft of the barn; in the afternoons she, her horse and her dog explored all the trails and back roads within thirty miles of that farm.

As a child, Laura dreamed of being a novelist, but as she grew older, her family's ties to England developed her interest in English history. After studying at the University of Michigan and at Yale, she became an historian and published articles and a book on Elizabethan literature and culture. Gradually escalating deafness, however, forced her to retreat to Vermont, where she began to write fiction for her two daughters (collectively, she and her husband now have seven children and fourteen grandchildren). Laura's book *Happily After All* and *The Island and the Ring* have been shortlisted for nine children's books awards and have been translated into Danish and German. *All the King's Horses* was her first book to be published by Corgi Books.

Laura and her husband, the poet F. D. Reeve, live in Vermont, where she teaches at Marlboro College. They have spent two years recently in London, where Laura has been working on a book about Victorian children's literature.